REVOLUTION

Revolution

Aaron Aalborg

Penman House Publishing

Published by Penman House Publishing

ISBN 978-0-9908764-0-3

Typesetting services by BOOKOW.COM

REVIEWS

"Revolution is an exciting and thought stimulating page turner. It is a dangerous book. I found myself in sympathy with much of its content and I am a retired and respectable history teacher."

"Unless this book is suppressed or sabotaged, it will take its place alongside other subversive, seditious and revolutionary tracts like those of Rousseau, Paine, Marx and Lenin."

"I abhor all violence and this novel cogently argues that bloody revolution is the only way to change the world for the better. The twist at the end purports to solve the problem of the revolutionaries turning into just another nasty power elite. Revolution is a deeply disturbing book. I wish I had not read it."

"Revolution stands directly opposed to Ayn Rand's 'Atlas Shrugged'. It appeals to those like me who feel that the very rich and powerful are simply luckier than most, by birth, genetic makeup or opportunity."

"Revolution should be banned! Its author should be imprisoned for incitement to terrorism. It purports to be a novel. It might seem so, to those who love action and suspense. In reality, it is a manual on how to cause and run a revolution. It is incitement to rebellion of the worst kind."

"Hey let's do it! This is long overdue."

DEDICATION

This book is dedicated to all those who have struggled and suffered in seeking equality and to overthrow dominance of the elites of their day. All had human foibles. Most fell victims to common misconceptions of their time, especially in religion or the practicality of communism. Many died for their beliefs and actions.

We need to remember that the Levellers, Chartists, Communists and early Socialists had few precedents from which to derive pragmatic solutions. They were acting on theories, many of which did not work in practice. Collectivization of farms is a good example, though its near relative, farming co-ops, work well enough.

On the other hand, few can read Emile Zola's Germinal without empathy. It is a novel about the misery, starvation and danger of working in the deep coalmines of north eastern France in the late 19th Century. The causes of that miners' strike and ultimate rebellion can be easily understood. In most developed countries things have improved from those times, but that did not just happen. Improvements had to be fought for. In the developing world conditions can be at least as bad as those described in Germinal.

The propaganda of the power elites of their time and the present day sullied and distorted the reputations of those listed below. A brief visit to the Internet for each of them is very rewarding. If that is too much, just look up those that you do not know or that you see as controversial choices. The following were selected as representative of various eras and to cover the globe. Many more were omitted. You may violently disagree with all or some of the choices.

Spartacus	Pádraig Pearce
William Wallace	José Francisco de San Martin
John Ball	Emiliano Zapata Salazar
Wat Tyler	Rosa Luxemburg
Jack Cade	Leon Trotsky
John Lilburne	Michael Collins
John Wildman	Patrice Lumumba
Tom Payne	Ernesto Che Guevara
Wolf Tone	Vilma Lucila Espin
Jean-Paul Marat	Phoolan Devi
Nelson Mandela	Aung San Suu Kyi

Donation to Charity

All profits from this book, if there are any, will be donated to Oxfam. This is a Charity that really gets aid quickly to those in need and has very low administrative costs. Visit the appropriate website to learn more about it. Give generously.

www.oxfam.org.uk/

www.oxfamamerica.org/

Acknowledgments

Thanks are due to a number of people who helped develop some of the ideas in this book or critiqued it at various stages. They bear no responsibility for the overall work and if Aaron Aalborg ends up in Guantanamo or more likely disappears suddenly, they should not be held responsible in any way for his activities.

Special thanks are due to K. Francis Ryan. He is the author of Echoes through the Mist, the first of the Echoes quartet. It is set in present day New York and Ireland and is the best novel I've read this year.

Echoes through the Vatican is set in present day Rome and is scheduled for release on December 1st of 2014. He has been especially helpful both in the development of Revolution and in preparing it for publication.

In addition, several others supported with editing, ideas and criticism, especially James Fraser; Ann Humphries, Dr. Solomon Moshe and Graeme Penman, who is an author and offers support services to authors

www.graemepenman.com

In Costa Rica, 'The Bards of Paradise' is a writers' group and its members have been especially helpful.

Michael Crump is the author of Candyman's War set in Guatemala during a brutal guerrilla war. His second novel is due out this fall and traces the journey of a family during the same period. He has published many short stories, which are available at

www.stillpointfiction.com.

Greg Bascom is the author of Lawless Elements, winner of the Faulkner-Wisdom gold medal for creative writing. It is a thrilling novel of intrigue and action in the struggle between the Philippine government and the Moros, the predominately Muslim tribes of the southern Philippines.

Hobbit Brown has written many short stories and is a poet. She helped with insights on entrepreneurial and political matters.

Dr. Lucinda Gray is a practicing psychologist and is the author of books on mindfulness; meditation and related subjects.

Dr. Lenny Karpman is a retired Cardiologist. He has authored many books on food, restaurants and travel.

Dr.Carol Marujo, a psychologist and educator, has devoted herself to peace activism, organic farming and writing in her retirement. She has published many freelance stories in The Tico Times, several magazines, and the anthologies Costa Rica Kaleidoscope and Wandering in Costa Rica. She is currently developing a cohousing community on her farm in the mountains.

My editor, Jim Parish, is a retired educator, who has a degree in English from Princeton. Jim did an excellent job of editing and offers such services to other writers. His email address is

costaricaslim@Yahoo.com

Lastly, I owe lasting gratitude to my long-suffering wife Ivy. She endured months of Aaron's ranting and fulminations. Sadly, this is a necessary part of my 'method' approach to writing. As in method acting, the author's alter ego becomes the main protagonist for the duration of writing. This can cause great concern, when revolutionary violence is the theme of the book in progress and irreversible schizophrenia seems imminent.

COVER DESIGN BY:

Alexandre Rito - www.designbookcover.pt

CHAPTER 1
DECAPITATE THE STATE!
CREATE CHAOS!

"The glories of our blood and state
Are shadows, not substantial things.
There is no armor against fate;
Death lays his icy hand on kings.
Scepter and crown
Must tumble down
And in the dust be equal made
With the poor crooked scythe and spade."

James Shirley 1596-1666

In a London hospital, a few years in the future

Mike, Lord Stoodley secretly spat out the tablets that the nurse gave him and pressed the button to elevate the back of his hospital bed. Its electric motor whined as the bed sat him up. A catheter drip fed medication into one arm. He stared at the TV screen intently with his good, ice blue eye. His identical glass eye was immobile in its socket. When it suited him to look piratical, he wore a black eye-patch. This lay on his bedside table, along with a water jug and an untouched bowl of fruit. He lost the eye to shrapnel, winning his Military Cross in the Falklands War between Britain and Argentina.

Peering through the sheer curtained window into the private room, the smartly suited female head of public relations for the hospital asked the duty nursing sister. "How's Lord Stoodley doing today, Sister?"

The head of PR thought to herself, *'We need to ensure that he's well looked after. He's tricky to handle. The press has him as a raffish and outspokenly popular military hero, politically connected and a corporate titan. We must avoid any bad publicity. Besides, high profile patients like him attract others of the same ilk.'*

The young ward sister frowned. "He's a very difficult and argumentative patient, but otherwise seems OK My nurses are all charmed by him and weak at the knees. You wouldn't think he was in his sixties. His body looks much younger. He must work out a lot."

"Ha, it sounds like you've been a little bit charmed, too."

The sister smiled, embarrassed. "Up to a point, all I get are demands for me to discharge him, so he can make it to Westminster Abbey for the funeral. We've mildly sedated him. He's so hyperactive."

"Well, as a man who's just had a heart attack, he needs to rest. Besides, the ceremony's already started. Look, he's watching it on TV. Your medications aren't working so well."

From Mike Stoodley's television, the bass notes of Bach's *All Men Are Mortal* reverberated through the forest of enormous organ pipes in Westminster Abbey. They resonated around the great 13th Century gothic cathedral as a somber background to the unctuous and over-deferential voice of the BBC commentator, which rose above the funereal music.

"There you can see the coffins of His Majesty the King; his heir, the much-loved Prince of Wales and the two pathetic tiny coffins of his children, the infant prince and princess. The monarch and the next three in line to the throne, all wiped out in one heinous tragedy. All are being honored in this single and historic state funeral today."

The camera zoomed out, away from the flag covered coffins. The camera's eye panned over the serried ranks of worthies from around the world, attending the funeral. The vast stone floor of the Abbey was packed to capacity. Rows of seats filled every space to accommodate them all. The camera then focused on individuals, as the silky Oxbridge tones of the BBC commentator continued.

"Here are the heads of state from around the world. All have come to show their solidarity with the British people and the grieving survivors from our Royal Family, victims of a horrible act of terrorism."

As the cameras moved on, "Now you see the President of the United States, her husband and the American Secretary of State. Normally US presidents never attend state funerals in foreign lands, but she was a close friend of the Prince of Wales. Next to her you can see the various monarchs and heads of state from the European Union. There is the Chancellor of Germany and next to him the President of the French Republic with his new wife, wearing a chic black hat and veil. Behind them are the various presidents and prime ministers of the British Commonwealth."

The US President had argued with her Secret Service head about making this trip. "Look! I'm the President and you don't tell me what to do, I tell you. There are as many risks in Washington as there are in the UK. Maybe Washington is the next target!" She had won her argument. She always did.

The BBC man went on, "See, there is the president of India in his white turban, sitting not too far from the president of Pakistan. For once they are united, in support of the British people in their mourning."

Off screen, he took a sip of water and carried on with his monologue, "Now we can see the president of Russia and the prime minister of the Peoples' Republic of China. The Chinese president is too frail to attend."

Those in the know, including the BBC team, surmised that the British Foreign Office blocked the invitation to the Dalai Lama. Getting the Chinese was considered more important.

"In these rows of seats are the world's religious leaders. There is the Pope in his distinctive white robes. His attendance at such an Anglican event is also a first, typical of this well-loved and reforming pontiff. Next to him is the head of the Russian Orthodox Church, the Patriarch of Moscow. Now we are focused on the Chief Rabbi, and various Muslim clerics. This sad event has truly brought together world leaders of every faith and political doctrine."

"There are many other Muslims here. They include the King of Saudi Arabia, the sultans of Oman, Brunei and the various United Arab Emirates, as well as the presidents of Egypt and Turkey, wearing their military dress uniforms. There is the new president of Syria. This occasion has united a troubled world in horror and deep respect."

The BBC man droned on and on. Stoodley was astonished that he could seemingly keep it up for hours, filling the gaps when nothing was happening with his signature snippets of British history and comments on royal protocol and precedent.

"The British Prime Minister and most of his cabinet are there on the right hand side of the nave, looking very solemn. Standing near them, grim faced, is leader of the opposition and his shadow cabinet."

From his hospital bed, Mike, Lord Stoodley, glanced expectantly at the large clock on the wall of his room and smiled thinly. As a member of the House of Lords, the UK's equivalent of the US Senate, Mike was entitled to be at the funeral. He chose to fake a heart attack instead. A couple of amphetamine tablets to temporarily speed his pulse and raise his blood pressure and complaining of shooting pains up his left arm and in his chest did the trick.

He balled his fists as he thought back to how he had battled his way into the British establishment, dwelling on the poverty and hardship that his family suffered. Whenever he wanted to reinforce his resolve, he did this. These thoughts were the rock on which his thirst for social justice was built. *'What is about to happen is right, just and necessary.'*

Mike knew that his time in the military provided a launch platform for his career as the entrepreneurial founder of a sprawling defense empire. He mused that this firm supplied mercenaries, contractors, security and military technology internationally to the UK, the US and approved allies. His discreet and close contacts with secret services and governments throughout the world were the envy of many. He was a billionaire, but lived modestly, deeply despising the glittering rich who called all the shots in the UK, the US and so much of the rest of the world.

When he was made a peer of the realm and member of the House of Lords, Mike chose the title 'Lord Stoodley' from his native Yorkshire. As a boy, he often hiked up the hill to the local stone landmark, Stoodley Pike, from his tiny family home in Todmorden. The Pike is a bleak 120-foot high stone pinnacle that broods over the desolate moorlands of the Pennine Hills.

On the rare hot summer days, he liked to sit in the cool shade of the monument and think how he might change the World. On the more common damp and windy days, he sheltered, white faced and shivering in the lea of the stone base of the pike, eating his cheese and pickle sandwiches from a tin lunch box.

Mike glanced at the clock again. The second hand swept its steady slow circle. He was tense with anticipation that at any minute, those that continued to rip-off and oppress the British people would receive their just desserts. The monitor pinged a slight quickening of his heartbeat.

Now riveted to the Television screen, he thought, *'Our intended targets are all present and correct. I was worried that the US President would go by precedent and send her Vice President instead of attending in person. Fortunately, the photo opportunities and the 24/7 attention of the world's media are too good for her to miss. She'll be planning side meetings with other leaders.'*

The funeral music switched to Mozart's *'Requiem'.* The BBC worthy prattled on, "This historic church, Westminster Abbey, was consecrated in 1065 on the orders of William the Conqueror. He promised such a magnificent edifice on the eve of the Battle of Hastings, if God granted him victory."

"Many of Britain's greatest monarchs are buried here. These include the great Henry V, a mighty warrior, immortalized by Shakespeare. The camera is showing our greatest playwright's memorial statue, which is here in the Abbey. It's life-sized. Shakespeare is sculpted wearing a cloak and is in the dress of the Elizabethan period.

"Our own tragically murdered Prince of Wales was in the same mould as Henry V. A decorated soldier, he fought in Afghanistan with his gallant brother. Here are also buried Henry VIII, founder of the Church of England, and his father Henry VII, the first Tudor King. Henry VIII's renowned and long reigning daughter, Queen Elizabeth I lies here too."

Mike sneered, knowing only too well that the 'Royal heroes' were well protected all the way in Afghanistan, at great risk to the lives of ordinary soldiers. Wearing a tailored uniform and playing with helicopters looked good for Royal PR, but hardly made them like Shakespeare's *Henry V*.

The BBC man spoke more softly, as if in a confidential aside, "A Westminster Abbey funeral is a break with recent tradition for the Royal House of Windsor. Its previous monarchs are all interred at Windsor Castle."

"Sadly, the Archbishop of Canterbury is not officiating today. His plane was delayed in South America, where he has been seeing his mother, who is Paraguayan. She is seriously ill. He will be with us in spirit. The ceremonies will be ably conducted by His Grace the Archbishop of York, second in the Church of England Hierarchy."

Finally more and more irritated by the smarmy BBC man, Mike Stoodley erupted, his face reddening. He spluttered in his bluff West Yorkshire accent, "Pompous, sycophantic overstuffed ass!"

His good eye flicked again to the clock and then to the TV screen. *'It must be any second now.'* His muscles tensed in the bed. *'Something can still go wrong.'* He felt the old anger welling up inside him. The hot blood throbbed in his temples. *"This one's for you dad and for you, Sarah."*

* * *

Colonel Johnny Hammond, officer commanding the large Special Air Service contingent for the funeral, sat in the vantage point of his command post. It was situated high in roof area of the Houses of Parliament; few knew of this room, accessed by a narrow oak staircase. He looked out on the twin gray stone towers that straddled the great front doors of Westminster Abbey, just across the street.

Hammond's earpiece chattered messages from the various sniper posts, providing security around the whole area. In his mind's eye, he pictured each of his thirty hand picked SAS troopers as they checked in. He saw each man, wearing black full combat equipment and body armor. The signature black balaclavas hid their faces. He could imagine each soldier perched in his position, earpiece and mike connected to the secure SAS radio network. He pictured the crosshairs of their sniper scopes, mounted on powerful rifles, roaming backwards and forwards across the crowds outside the Abbey.

Some troopers were hidden, high in the roof, inside the Abbey itself. They scrutinized those attending far below. One, a sergeant, reminded himself, *'These days, you never know where a threat might come from.'* He even studied the gold braided, bright scarlet and blue uniforms of the highly decorated senior military guests and the smart dress uniforms of the guard of honor around the coffins. They stood out amongst the mass of dignitaries in their black mourning garb. *'Could any of them be wearing an explosive vest?'*

Hammond glanced over the bank of monitors streaming CCTV pictures from cameras all around the area outside and inside the Abbey. The latest Israeli-supplied facial recognition and analysis software constantly scanned the faces of the throng, seeking potential threats. As each face appeared, it froze the image, drawing straight lines joining points on its key features. In less than a second, it compared each face to the tens of thousands of known and suspected terrorists, seeking a match. It also looked for telltale micro expressions of fear, anger and malicious intent.

Hammond stood up to ease his cramped legs and nervously peered out of the small window again. He took in the unprecedented size of the masses, in the streets around the Abbey.

Below in these streets, the British people, incensed by the outrageous slaughter of the King and heirs to the throne, had turned out in their hundreds of thousands. They stood in reverent silence, listening to the broadcast proceedings over the many loudspeakers.

Hammond turned back to his screens commenting to his second in command. "Remember the funeral of Princess Diana? This is much bigger."

His mind wandered from his task, *'We Brits do this kind of thing better than anyone else. He looked at a close up of the French president in the Abbey on another monitor. He's positively green with envy, miserable little Frog'.*

As a history graduate from Oxford, Hammond knew very well that the British Royal line had many unseemly breaks. He remembered snippets from his studies, *'Henry VII had an unlikely and convoluted claim to the throne. George I spoke only German and was 52nd in line of succession. He was the only semi-presentable protestant available at the time. Catholics were hated back then.'*

He smiled, thinking, *'What am I doing here? The present "Royal" line of British monarchs has minimal legitimacy and is mostly of German ancestry. They're merely figureheads. The current lot are toffee-nosed and stupid from too much in-breeding. Despite the poor raw material, their public relations machine serves them well. In the days of the Raj, the Royals slaughtered hundreds of tigers. Even now they annually massacre thousands of deer, grouse and pheasants bred for the purpose on their huge estates. Yet they are portrayed as wanting to save endangered species. It's just ludicrous.'*

He further mused, *'For anything like this, the British people suddenly love Royalty. The Royals are a gilded soap opera for the often-prurient entertainment of our populace. There's nothing the Brits like better than a Royal birth, a funeral or a salacious scandal. There've been many juicy scandals.'*

Despite his cynicism, a lump of pride formed in Hammond's throat. *'We Brits can still put on a full pomp and circumstance show to beat anyone.*

'It's funny how those without enthroned Royals of their own, the Yanks, the Germans and the French, find ours so fascinating. They all come and bow and curtsey. This funeral has a worldwide TV audience of hundreds of millions. If I screw up, I'll never live it down!'

He felt a little guilty for his thoughts. *'As a soldier, my duty is to protect the legitimate government and monarchy of the United Kingdom, no matter how archaic some of its traditions and despite the rank stupidity of most of its current leaders.'*

Pulling himself back to his professional self, he puffed out his chest and addressed the room at large and his troopers on the secure net. "Keep sharp everybody! We've had more than enough terrorism for one month."

He concealed his unease from his men. *'How did those bastards get away with murdering our king? Maybe they are here below somewhere. What will they do next?'*

* * *

Two weeks earlier, the highly polished and discretely, but heavily armored Rolls Royce, carrying the king; his son and heir, the Prince of Wales as well as his two young grandchildren, drove from Windsor Castle towards Buckingham Palace. On a clear spring morning with blue skies and unseasonably warm temperatures, the convoy drove at some speed. The king enjoyed teasing his grandchildren about the planned birthday party for the young prince, later that day.

As always, security was tight. The pilot and observer in the circling dark blue police helicopter had only received the final route and exact time ten minutes previously. The same applied to the Royal entourage and its protective escort.

The chopper's observer saw no crowds, only the curious odd passer-by glimpsing the flashing blue lights on the motorcycle outriders and the fast moving stream of large black vehicles. An upturned white face stared at the clattering helicopter.

As the chopper crew watched, the cars sped up the ramp of the overpass at Hammersmith, known locally as the Flyover. High modern office buildings flanked the overpass, hives buzzing with hundreds of office workers settling at their computer monitors for a day's toil.

Without warning, an enormous flash erupted from the center of the flyover. The pilot flinched and instinctively gripped the controls. He banked away as fast as he could. The shock wave violently shook and spun the chopper, enveloping the entire area and shattering the surrounding office buildings. Even a mile away, the blast was deafening. A mushroom cloud of dust and falling debris rapidly obscured the scene. It was minutes before the chopper crew could discern anything and then only dimly through a grey dust cloud.

In the murk below, the entire convoy lay shattered. Most of the vehicles, mangled and twisted beyond recognition, had been hurled many feet. Some lay intact, upside down and on fire.

It took fifteen minutes for the first emergency response vehicles to weave their way in through the debris. Police, fire and ambulance crews clambered over blackened lumps of tangled ferroconcrete. They struggled to breathe through their oxygen gear. Finally, they reached the still burning royal car on the collapsed overpass. All the surrounding offices showed heavy damage. Dead and injured employees were strewn everywhere. Others, deafened by the blast and covered in dust and blood, sat slumped amongst the debris in shocked horror.

Colonel Johnny Hammond recalled that when the death toll was eventually rendered, there were over a hundred and fifty fatalities and more than three hundred seriously injured. Many would not survive. Over a hundred others were still unaccounted for.

* * *

Jack Brewer, the enigmatic and no nonsense head of the Special Branch of the Metropolitan Police and a respected colleague of Colonel Johnny Hammond, led the subsequent briefing to the investigating team of senior military, police and members of the government. Twenty of them sat around a large table in a secure bunker in Whitehall. The more junior members perched on smaller chairs behind them. Jack sipped from a glass of water. Then grim faced, he said, "There are no leads on the perpetrators of the royal murders. Those terrorists are still out there. Dealing with the forensic evidence from the mile square crime site might take months."

"All we have so far is that military grade explosives were used. Forensics narrowed it down to C4. As you know, this type of explosive is in widespread use within NATO. It is light, powerful and easy to use. Shaped charges of C4 below the central spans of the flyover caused catastrophic damage. Placing them took some time and quite a few people."

Hammond sat forward in his chair at the far end of the table and interrupted, "Damn it all Jack, someone must have seen something! How could they possibly stash that much explosive and wire it up under the Flyover without anyone noticing?"

Jack said, "I'd think that too. CCTV from the area and all information about some contractors working under the bridge a week before has mysteriously vanished. People remember the scaffolding and orange work overalls, but little else. So far, there's nothing to suggest that foreign terrorists were involved. We know of no one outside the forces of the major powers, capable of doing this."

"It was a clever place to lay an ambush. Most routes from Windsor to Buck Palace include the Flyover. But how did they know the timing? That's the key question. They must have someone on the inside!"

Shortly afterwards, at the top level briefing in 10 Downing Street, Hammond heard Jack telling the prime minister, "The CIA, Mossad and intelligence services of the European allies have picked up nothing on this.

The usual terrorist groups are excited by it now, but don't seem to be involved."

Hammond thought, *'No wonder Jack and Special Branch are worried. The enemy is unknown, highly capable and still out there.'*

* * *

The Royal Funeral was in progress. Peering through the thick laminated glass of his bullet-proof window overlooking the Abbey, Hammond brought his attention back to the task in hand. He glanced up at the three matt black helicopter gunships carrying his mobile force, as they circled a thousand feet above. *'Let's hope all will be well. I've done all I can.'*

Despite this, the hairs on the back of his neck erected, something did not feel right. He looked nervously at his monitors.

* * *

A short while earlier, twenty miles to the North near the town of Hertford, Sheila Reynolds' ministerial Jaguar sped down a narrow and twisting country lane, with its two escorting unmarked police Range

Rovers. She was Britain's Home Secretary, responsible for all U.K. police forces.

The maroon Jaguar hurtled round a corner, closely following the lead Range Rover. From a farm gate, as if from nowhere, a large green tractor lurched into the road. It missed the lead Range Rover, smashing into Sheila's car. The Jag slewed across the road, slammed into the hedge and jerked her forwards against her safety belt. Her driver, who never wore a belt, smashed his head into the windscreen. Blood ran down his shattered face and he was unconscious. Hissing steam erupted from the broken radiator. The Front Range Rover screeched to a halt, leaving a mark of scorched rubber. The following vehicle, tires squealing, stopped in time to just miss the Jaguar. Detective Sergeant Daniels, temporary head of her security detail, leapt out and tore open her door. His team was already trying to help her chauffer. In the chaos, they missed the driver of the tractor slipping away behind the hedge in the field and into a spinney.

Sheila, her adrenalin up and eyes flashing, ranted at her minders. "How could you be so stupid? I saw that tractor coming from fifty yards away and I was in the fucking back seat!"

In public, she was all sweetness and smiles. In private she was a harridan. Her foul language was all the more cutting, due to her Oxford University drawl.

Sergeant Daniels clamped his lips tight. Suppressing his rising anger he thought, *'You absolute bitch! I'd like to strangle you. It's only a damned traffic accident. Even trained police drivers have 'em occasionally and you insisted on coming this way to see the countryside and then we were late!'*

Sheila Reynolds had a reputation as a ball breaker. Her blond good looks and gentle smile simply lured her victims within range. Emolliently, Daniels pointed out. "We could still make the funeral, if you allow me to call in the duty helicopter."

"And how the fuck would that look on the TV? **'The Home Secretary leaves her badly injured driver and other accident victims to flee the scene!'"**

"Anyway, get the TV on in the back of your car. The funeral will start soon. I'm staying here to watch it."

She settled her fattening rump into the comfortable rear seat of the sergeant's Range Rover to view the funeral on the small screen in the back of the seat in front of her. She relaxed just a little. *'My cover story for not being in the Abbey is in place. It'll be time soon.'* She checked her watch, as the second hand swept away the minutes.

* * *

When it came, the blast was overwhelming. In his HQ, in The Houses of Parliament, the wall and armored glass window in front of Colonel Johnny Hammond blew inwards.

Everything seemed to happen in slow motion as his adrenalin kicked in. He received a massive jolt to his chest when his body armor caught the impact of shards of glass and chunks of masonry. He felt sharp cuts as glass splinters slashed his face.

He lay on his back, deafened. Blood trickled into his eyes and down his cheeks. A piercing pain wracked his arm. He wiped his eyes with his other hand. *'My arm, it must be broken. I must stay conscious.'* In despair, he glimpsed dust, bodies and chaos all around him.

* * *

The CNN helicopter, with its powerful, stabilized telephoto camera, circled outside the three-mile exclusion zone, that the Brits had set up to keep the press back. It transmitted a live broadcast of the best shots of the enormous explosion that blew Westminster Abbey and all those in it to smithereens. The flash and smoke filled TV screens all over the world.

The shock wave pitched the chopper into a violent spin. The pilot wrestled with his controls, revving the throttles to stay airborne. The news reporter, with the scoop of his lifetime, stammered his shocked commentary in a voice choking with emotion,

"Oh my God! This is unbelievable. The church is gone. Oh Lord have mercy, the president is in there! This is terrible. Oh, the tragedy!"

He sobbed hysterically, as his pilot abruptly swerved into a wider circuit to escape the billowing dust cloud. Below, they saw the crowds stampeding and trampling over each other in panic. The on-board camera captured a series of further explosions rippling along the surrounding streets. It looked as though they were all erupting from beneath the roadways. Some manhole covers and bodies hurtled upwards and spurts of explosive flame leapt from the ground. They saw thousands of panicked Londoners and tourists being shredded.

Ten seconds later, all UK civilian telephones, TV signals and the Internet went dead. Millions of half-typed texts and tweets were interrupted.

* * *

In his control bunker a few hundred yards away, Special Branch Commander Jack Brewer gasped in horror. Then his banks of monitoring screens went blank. A sinister message came over the supposedly secure line into his earpiece in an electronically modified and emotionless voice. "You can't resist, Jack. We hear all your communications. Go home to your Megan and your daughter Joan. Give up, or you'll all die!"

Then this line too went dead. Jack gasped, frightened for his family, then steeled himself, *'The hell with that! We'll get you bastards, if it's the last thing we do!'*

He asked himself. *'Who did this and why? They must have had internal help. When we can answer that question we can begin to fight back. The problem is what to do now? I must do something. Where should I go?'*

CHAPTER 2
THE SEEDS OF DESTRUCTION

"If you tremble in indignation at every injustice, then you are a comrade of mine."

Ernesto 'Che' Guevara, Argentinean, a hero
to revolutionaries, murdered after capture
in Bolivia, on the orders of the CIA.

Freshers' Day on the Campus of the University of Essex near Colchester England, 1967

17-year-old Mike, from the sooty and industrially blighted town of Todmorden in Yorkshire, picked his way nervously through the throng of noisy and bemused new students. Walking nervously between the stalls of the various university clubs and societies, he felt confused. A tug at his sleeve arrested his step.

It was a weird looking guy, manning one of the stalls. He looked earnestly at Mike, desperately trying to recruit some of this year's freshers. Mike brushed him off and moved to a corner, where he could gather his thoughts and be less conspicuous.

The sheer number and variety of offerings overwhelmed him. Mike noted that most stalls and other students seemed to be of a political bent. He saw many gaudy, screen-printed posters. Hand painted banners adorned the various stalls. Scanning the charmless concrete paved square, he spotted some drunken students falling into the fountain. He chuckled quietly, as others even merrier pushed them in. A few dragged their mates in after them. They noisily splashed and floundered about in their attempts to get out. Those nearby moved back to avoid getting wet.

Some of his fellow freshers surprised Mike. Gaggles of hippies looked as though they had come straight from San Francisco. He remembered seeing such exotic creatures on his parents' black and white TV. In the flesh, the bright colors of their clothes seemed even more bizarre. He noticed that they were wreathed in a seemingly permanent cannabis haze.

The girls wore flowing dresses. They had garlands around their long straight hair, which hung down their backs. Some were stunningly attractive and obviously braless under the clinging fabrics. The boys sported tie-died t-shirts and bell-bottomed jeans with large flower motifs. Their hair was long or in the fuzzy Afro style. Many affected bandanas and John Lennon moustaches.

As some paraded past Mike, their language sounded strange, delivered in slow dreamy drawls. He heard lots of, "Hey, man! Cool! Far out!"

Many students had formed pairs and groups already. His shoulders slumped a little because he felt very much out of things and utterly alone.

Taking a breath, he squared his shoulders and dived back into the throng. He could tell from their accents that most of his fellow students came from the southern England that he hardly knew and vaguely resented. He had never met anyone from the South in Todmorden, but popular opinion, as voiced by his Uncle Sam was, "They're effete; talk funny and always on the make. Spivs, the lot of 'em!"

His dad was even more damning, "Thi can't hold their weak southern beer."

Mike thought one lad looked exactly like the popular leftist icon Che Guevara. He clearly cultivated the look, with his beard and black Che beret. He even smoked a cheroot. Presumably the big cigars favored by Che were too expensive on a student's budget. Mike saw this lad's look reflected in the many posters of an idealized Che around the square. The red and black screen printed posters of the hero stared defiantly down from the various concrete pillars. Some students wore similar images printed on their t-shirts.

In his scruffy jeans and long sideburns, Mike had not expected these alien people, in their strange cliques and weird clothes. He had never seen a hippy in the Todmorden of 1967. Revolutionary socialists were unheard of in the pubs and workingmen's clubs that he frequented. He felt lost, uncharacteristically nervous and unsophisticated.

Another shock to Mike's vision of Essex came when he talked to the students manning the stalls. They seemed much more knowledgeable and part of the scene or at least pretended to be.

Of course, he had read the works of Tom Paine, Hobbs, Rousseau, Marx and his particular favorite, George Orwell. These weirdoes spouted quotations from Bakunin, Trotsky, Regis Debray and Che. It seemed all a bit affected. Nonetheless, they sounded much better suited to this strange new world outside of Todmorden than he was.

Mike began to wonder why he chose Essex. He recalled the university's glossy prospectus emphasizing modernity, with a heavy focus on the social sciences. Now he felt as though he was wandering through some kind of extraterrestrial zoo. Troops of splendidly colored animals swaggered about in colorful parade. He tried to merge into the background, strangely isolated and unable to compete.

Mike surmised that the faux Che character must be joining the School of Latin American Studies. From the prospectus he recalled *'Essex is the only university in Britain offering degrees in Latin American Politics.'* He remembered that it boasted 'a full term's course in revolution.'

Happily he noted the especially active stalls recruiting for various leftist groups. A lonely, shorthaired Conservative Party member stood bedraggled at his stall. He had just had a beer poured over him. *'Good job, too!'* thought Mike.

* * *

The previous day Mike arrived at Essex by bus, carrying his worldly possessions in a couple of heavy canvas bags, and a huge chip on his shoulder, derived from his heritage and family background.

On arrival, he shut himself in the Spartan room assigned to him, threw himself on the narrow bed and closed his eyes. As he often did when he felt out of things and needed reorientation, he retreated to the touchstone of his strongest memories.

His grandfather spent a lot of time with Mike when he was young, sharing stories of strikes and the near starvation of the 1920s and 30s. Mike listened attentively, his young mind trying to grasp the hardships of love on the dole and the socialism that would change all that. Mike's grandmother, deafened from a lifetime serving her four clattering looms in the weaving shed, told him "We started work up at mill at age nine. We had half a day for schoolin. At twelve, we wus working full time and long hours."

These things mattered to Mike. He cast his mind back, remembering being twelve and fascinated as his father told his WWII stories. "Remember this, Son. The Japs were fanatics. They felt it was honorable to die for their emperor. They overran much of Asia, includin' all our colonies in the South, Malaya and Burma. They were cruel and merciless devils. They bayoneted our wounded, beheaded prisoners and worked others to death on starvation rations. Remember that film I took you to see, 'The Bridge on the river Kwai.' That's what it were like. Never buy anythin' Japanese, Son. It's all cheap rubbish anyhow!"

Dad told him of life operating behind the Jap lines in Burma, of malaria and beriberi; living on meager rations; of the ubiquitous, blood-sucking leaches and the cruelty of a merciless, cunning enemy. "After suffering all that in the war, we was demobbed. We expected a fresh start, *'a land fit for heroes'*, they told us. Same thing they spouted to yer granddad after the First World War."

"We was all bleedin' 'eros when there was fightin' to be done, but nothing as soon as it wus all over. Instead, all the best civilian jobs went to them in the officer class, just like before. I had to take a laborer's job in the spinning mill."

* * *

A year later, 13 year old Mike sat at his desk in the crowded schoolroom. A man knocked on the glass window of the door. Fierce Mr. Hardcastle, the teacher, looked over testily. Then he strode over to open it. Mike and his classmates craned their necks to see who was interrupting the lesson. He saw his dad's foreman from the mill, cloth cap in hand, deferentially talking to the teacher. They both looked serious.

Mr. Hardcastle took Mike aside, "Something bad's happened at the factory. You'd best get up to the hospital right away."

***

Mike sat by his father's bedside in the public ward of the local hospital. He had called in at home on the way. His mother was incoherent and in tears. Her disjointed wailing made no sense. There had been some sort of accident in the mill.

The bossy matron told Mike nothing, when he asked her about his dad, "You'll have to ask him that. You can only stay 'alf an hour. Ee's still very weak."

Dad lay back in bed, deathly pale. He had lost his strong and confident voice. "Both mi legs are gone, Son. I slipped and was dragged into the conveyor for the wool bales. The chain driving it chewed up both legs. They had to take 'em off. Those bastards at t'mill are already sayin' it were my fault, but it weren't."

Mike cried as his dad told him, "The accident 'appened because the unguarded conveyor dragged me into its mechanism, after mi foot slipped on a greasy floor."

***

A few years later, now seventeen, Mike tossed his school books on the kitchen table. His mum had a complete mental breakdown and was in a secure institution. Now it was just him and his dad. The mill owners had paid out very little in compensation. Their insurers said it was 'an act of God'.

Mike had prepared bread and cheese for his dad's tea. "Dad, where are you?"

There was no answer, so he went into the front room, where his dad usually sat up in bed. He saw the empty bed, with a dent in the pillow and the sheets pulled back. The back door swung open in the chill winter wind.

Mike looked into their tiny back yard, with just enough room for an outside privy, a small bunker for the coal fire and the round metal rubbish bin with its fitted lid.

He remembered how his dad lay there on his face, wearing his night shirt. The earth around his head was dark and wet. Mike thought he must have fallen trying to get to the privy on his leather-encased stumps and maybe banged his head.

Worried, Mike ran over to him trying to lift him up by the shoulder. His dad's head flopped down. Mike jumped back in horror. He felt as though someone kicked him in the stomach and winded him.

Blood had spurted everywhere. Dad had a huge open slash across his neck. His long, mother-of-pearl handled razor lay open and smeared with blood next to his limp, death-white and stone-cold hand. Mike had often watched him stropping the razor to a sharp edge on the thick piece of leather that hung from a nail on the wall. His dad forbade him to touch it. "Tha'll cut thi sen."

Later he found the suicide note in an envelope on the mantelpiece and held it in his shaking hands.

> *"Dear Mike,*
>
> *I care too much to be any more of a burden.*
> *Being crippled is no life for a man.*
> *Caring for a cripple is no life for you.*
> *I did my best.*
>
> *Remember me, but remember the class war*
> *that you need to fight.*
> *You will find a way, when the time comes.*
>
> *I love you.*
> *Dad"*

Mike kept those words in his heart forever. Deep in his being, they lit the white hot and unquenchable fire of rebellion.

* * *

On the eve of Freshers' Day, Mike checked into his 14th floor student accommodation in Raleigh Tower. The four accommodation towers were the tallest brick buildings in Europe. He liked the rather monkish, stark white painted brick walls of his small room. The room was furnished with a narrow bed, a clothes rail and a tiny, built-in desk with an integral bookshelf of polished pine. Showers, toilets and a kitchen were shared with the other eight young men, housed in the apartment. They seemed as nervous and lost as he, though some pretended not to be.

There were also a couple of study rooms on each floor, each used by four students who officially slept away from the Wivenhoe campus. They often dossed down on the floor of the study in sleeping bags. The rooms smelt of stale sweat and cannabis smoke.

Mike shut the outside world out from his room as he closed the door. He let his angry memories run wild.

The new University of Essex, with its freshly made liberal prospectus, was going to be the place for him. He wanted to learn and never work in the mills, if there were any left after recent closures. Maybe he could become a union official or get a job in government where he could help the needy and oppressed.

As far as he was concerned, old Etonians, Harrovians and the undeserving inherited aristocracy still ruled Britain.

* * *

Now, only one day later, disillusion set in. Seeing the reality of the university on Freshers' Day, he felt alone and out of place. He thought, *"Have I made a mistake? Everything is so strange. These middle class posers aren't my folk.'*

At seventeen, Mike was a staunch supporter of the British Labour Party. With his working class background, how could he be anything else? In Todmorden, all his neighborhood playmates had known hard times. They lived very closely together in the rows of insanitary and cold terraced houses. The damp walls grew black mold. Many of the neighbors had chest complaints, spitting up black phlegm at frequent intervals.

Due to the soot and grime from the hundreds of mill chimneys and coal fires in the houses, those built of cheap brick were hard to distinguish from those built from the once yellow Yorkshire stone. A house was always just black. Even the grand Victorian, stone mansions belonging to the mill owners were covered in grime. They had fancy gardens and views looking down on their mills, their workers' houses and the town that they controlled.

In the meanest houses below, though the people were poor, each front step was swept daily and rubbed bright ochre with a soft 'holystone'. These were prized and provided by the rag and bone man in exchange for old clothes, or perhaps a battered, twisted bicycle frame or sometimes for a rusted and broken pram.

The kids used to laugh and follow his open cart, pulled by a mangy pony, as the dirty and raggedy driver, hunched over the reins and shouted, "Rag a bone! Rag a bone!"

If the boys got too cheeky, the man might shout, "Booger off!" and jerk his pony into a trot, to escape the little pests.

* * *

Mike was stirred from his thoughts at the freshers' event by a shout. "Hey there, sideburns, where're ya goin?"

Mike looked round the crowded square to see a pudgy and cheery faced lad with stubble and bug eyes. He wore a dirty black T shirt with holes in it and equally tired and frayed jeans. It was Jerry, one of his new flat mates from his student accommodation tower, one of four built so far. He only met him the day before and liked him instantly. He was a good laugh. Mike rejoined, "Goin fer a pint. Wanna come?"

Nursing their pints of Newcastle Brown Ale in the student bar, they shared confidences. Jerry told Mike that he was Jewish, from the working class East end of London. His father fought the fascist black shirts in the street fights of the 1930s. Jerry grew up on the fringe of London's criminal gangs. "I saw the Kray twins in our local pub a few times."

Being in the milieu of London's most infamous gangsters lent Jerry an aura of being street wise. The Kray twins were widely covered in the popular newspapers. They had grown up in the poor East End of London and had emerged as amateur boxers, before taking to a life of crime, terror and murder.

Mike sensed a kindred spirit in Jerry. Before long, both lads discovered that drinkers from more privileged backgrounds were all around them. One, Mungo Hopton, had even been to Eton, the exclusive and expensive private school attended by most of Britain's prime ministers and most of its cabinet members, for over two hundred years. It had strange customs like boys wearing top hats and a school song in

Latin, 'The Carmen Etonense'. Boys there still learned Latin as well as Ancient Greek.

Mungo spoke with a braying drawl. "I say, Rupert old chap, come and have a gin and T with me and Cynthia."

Another had a high-powered sports car. It was a canary yellow Jaguar XK150. Jessica and Helen, two spectacular and willowy blonds, constantly hung around his neck. He spoke little. He had no need. Needless to say, sexual jealousy caused Mike and Jerry to take an instant dislike to him.
"Bleedin wanker!" Jerry commented.

* * *

At his Yorkshire grammar school, Mike was seen as the rebel. He was much disliked and often thrashed by the headmaster; nasty Mr. Hardcastle and by most of the other teachers. Canings were usually at least once a week, but casual slaps, slipperings, wrenching of sideburns and painful ear tuggings were a daily routine.

Harry Newton, the tough ex paratrooper who taught Physical Education, was the only teacher Mike respected. He brought out the best in him, including his ability to box much bigger boys. Mike learned to endure grueling long distance runs through the heather, across marshy tracks and through the dank chilling mists, sharp rushes and black, boy-swallowing peat bogs of the West Yorkshire Moors.

Much to the chagrin of his teachers, Mike earned the best academic results of his final year. He received scholarship offers from several universities. To his harassed teachers it seemed unfair that an unruly and outspoken lad had done so well. Mr. Hardcastle complained to those in his staff room. "That little tyke is too cheeky by half. He'll come to a bad end. You mark my words!"

At the end of the school year, Mike skipped the school prize giving, speechifying and handing out of examination certificates. He thought, *'Stuff em all! I'll be goin' to Uni soon and then I'll show 'em.'*

* * *

Jerry and Mike strolled around the Essex campus, before dinner. The University was set in the green of the landscaped parkland, with its attractive lake. The original 18th Century Wivenhoe House was once a grand manor on the edge of the park. Now it was used by the university administration. The new buildings of the university were crammed together into one corner of the park. Their pale concrete and glass disrupted the tranquility of the landscape, like an intrusive alien space city.

The new students could see that many buildings were still under construction. Aside from the four towers were the massive and stark concrete buildings, housing lecture theaters, canteens and administration blocks. The architecture was heavy handed and block house grey. Mike commented on the Hexagon, housing the canteen and large meeting room to Jerry. "Look, it's like the turret of some enormous battleship. It's slab sided. The tiny vertical windows emphasize the thickness of the construction, giving it the illusion of having heavy armor plate."

The attempts at making the light grey concrete look friendlier utterly failed. In a courtyard, the square pond and rough texturing of the pillars with crude fluting just added to the gloomy atmosphere.

Mike had read that experiments with rats living in similar high-density groups led them to rape, cannibalism and vicious fighting. He thought, *'If the architects had only known this they could have predicted the place's current reputation for anarchy and dissent.'*

Like many others, an unhappy Mike ended his Freshers' Day dead drunk and stoned in the bar. Though he was a few months below legal drinking age, no one checked. Why would they when the whole place was wreathed in clouds of hashish smoke? The police durst not venture on to the campus. The liberal vice chancellor had persuaded the chief constable to leave them alone.

At closing time, Mike stumbled off to his tower, swaying between two new friends from Raleigh 14. Somehow, he had signed up earlier for a few student clubs. Beside the Karate Club, he was now in the Theater Arts Society and the Film Society. They promised programs of radical and arts films and avant-garde plays.

He also joined the university Labour Party Club. He was disappointed and puzzled at how few students seemed to be in the latter. He soon found out why. The Labour Party was at best considered as middle of the road. Essex students had drastically more radical politics.

At least Labour had more members than in the Conservative Club. Jerry explained. "They have only four members and everyone hates them."

They had enjoyed the satisfaction of seeing the be -suited student Tory chairman tossed into the fountain, after the earlier beer pouring incident. Essex was no place for Conservatives. That boy must have had a deep masochistic streak.

Mike wondered what he has let himself in for, but was excited by the prospects.

* * *

In December 1967 Mike was at a party in the ancient small port of Wivenhoe. The house was better furnished than most student digs. There was gin and whisky available. Most parties were 'bring your own' affairs. Funds might run to beer or cider.

As usual, he was pretty drunk and lonely. He watched the colored lights throb to the wild music of Cream's 'N.S.U.' Suddenly he was pulled into a corner at the foot of the stairs by a plumpish girl with light brown hair. She clamped her lips to his mouth. He tasted the hashish on her flickering tongue and lips. He smelled the shampoo on her light brown hair. As he gasped for breath, her left leg wrapped around him like a tendril. He felt the hot flesh of her inner thigh. As she pressed her breasts against him, he could feel that she was not wearing underwear.

Frenziedly, she pushed her hot tongue deep into his throat, pressing her hardening nipples against him.

They had frenetic sex on the staircase. Afterwards, she looked dreamily at him and said, "I'm Sheila Reynolds. What's your name?"

She had seemed pretty high on something, but most people at parties were. He wondered whether he would see her again. She had kicked him out in the early hours so she could sleep, with a slap on his rump and a determined, "That's it for tonight! Off you go home now, lover boy." Maybe, she was a bit bossy and posh for him, but 'free love' at university was not as widely available as the gutter press reported.

* * *

Bleary eyed, Sheila awoke with tousled hair amongst her love tangled sheets. She had a splitting hangover. She struggled into her robe and swerved round the half empty beer glass on the stairs. She kicked a deadbeat, sleeping on the floor in the sitting room and grumped at him. "Back to your place now, Freddy!"

He groaned at her, "Shit, Sheila you're a hard woman."

She surveyed the detritus of the party in the kitchen. "Fuck!" she exclaimed, her headache pounding. Her nose wrinkled at the sour, sickly smells of stale beer, sweat and smoke. She threw open a window.

Sipping the freshness of a chilled, restorative orange juice she smiled at the warm memory of Mike. He was a rough lout, but he had a tight little bum and strong arms. Besides his Yorkshire accent and pukka working class background would certainly build credibility with her socialist friends. She hoped he would call her.

CHAPTER 3
THE BOY FROM PARAGUAY

"Religion is regarded by the common people as true, by the wise as false, and by the rulers as useful."

Lucius Annaeus Seneca

Phil Saunders had a very different experience of the Freshers' gathering at Essex. The day before he had sat in his off campus digs, reflecting on his childhood.

His dad had been a Church of England missionary, the youngest of the three sons of the Bishop of Bath and Wells. As such, his father had a privileged up-bringing. His childhood home was the historic 800-year old Bishop's Palace, next to Wells Cathedral in Somerset. Following in the Bishop's footsteps, his dad became a pious member of the Church of England. He took Holy Orders, after an education in a British public school and, unusually, a Doctorate in Divinity from a university in New Mexico.

Phil recalled his dad telling him, "Most missionaries from the UK go to our former and remaining colonies, especially in Africa. There, they wean the locals from their pagan superstitions and onto our true Christian beliefs."

Now, Phil mused, *'It was a case of trading their superstitions for ours. It started with the land belonging to the tribes and the missionaries shipping in tea chests full of bibles. Before long, the tribes had the bibles and the white settlers owned the land, a clever little scam.'*

Phil's father, the Reverend Saunders, was sent to Paraguay instead of Africa. He told Phil how it had happened. "This posting was due to my fluency in Spanish and partly to my US education. After a spell in a parish at home in Southern England, an old US college friend phoned me, *'Hey, how'd you like to run a mission station in Paraguay? Our US Anglican Church has one in a village near a town called Dr. Pedro P. Peña. It's in the Chaco region.'*

His dad told him he replied, "Wow, Joe! That's a bit out of the blue. Why me? What a funny name for a place and I've never heard of the Chaco region."

"We thought of you because you speak some Spanish and you did well in the US. People liked you. You seem up for the adventure and are resourceful."

"The town is named for a long forgotten Ministro of the Interior. It's in the far western part of Paraguay, near the border with Argentina. There are indigenous people up there. They've not yet heard The Word."

So his father went to Paraguay and married Consuela, his mother. She was one of Dad's parishioners. Phil was born in Wells during a rare family vacation in the UK.

Phil's happy memories of his early years in Paraguay centered round their literally dirt poor village, with its single, rutted and dusty street, a quagmire when it rained. There was a small Anglican school with a sod roof and a tiny white-washed mission church.

Chickens and other animals roamed between and often into the humble mud brick houses. These were without sanitation. The floors were of hardened earth, but were swept clean each day.

The grander haciendas of the landowners had tin or tiled roofs. They were situated on their surrounding farming or hunting estates. Phil had only heard of these luxurious places, but had seen the entrances to some. The landowners stuck with their old Catholic religion, if they had any religion at all. Most of them only paid lip service to it.

Their properties had archways with closed gates over their approach roads. Stern men with guns chased away Phil and any other inquisitive urchins. If caught, they were beaten. The haciendas were out of sight, far in the distances beyond the forbidding gates

Phil was bilingual in Spanish and English. He played well with the local children. Because he was good at soccer, the national sport and obsession, he was popular. Like the rest of the boys, he played 'fútbol' without shoes on their parched 'cancha'. Such rural soccer pitches, together with a church, a school and maybe a bar and a general store, formed the cultural centers of every small village in Latin America.

As he grew to be more aware, he learned that land ownership in rural areas dictated wealth and was heavily concentrated. Hungry for information, Phil read his father's weeks' old newspapers in Spanish and listened to local gossip and rumors.

He discovered that Generalísimo Presidente Alfredo Stroessner ran Paraguay with an iron fist. With the backing of the United States, Stroessner staged a military coup in 1954 and installed a fascist and strongly

anti-communist regime. Stroessner kept a low profile. This limited publication of what was really going
on.

Nonetheless, even this far from the capital, it was
known that only members of El Presidente's 'Partido
Colorado' were eligible for highly paid jobs. To argue
was to be roughed up or even to disappear. Conversations about such matters were in hushed tones and
only within the family or between trusted friends. Informers or orejas (ears) were everywhere.

Phil knew from his father that many fugitives from
Nazi Germany found safe haven in Latin America
after WWII. Argentina, Chile and Paraguay were favored destinations. This was partly due to their existing German communities, many of which welcomed
their heroes. The right wing governments of Peron,
Pinochet and Stroessner were sympathetic to the
Nazis. Their regimes mirrored their fascist prede-
cessors in Europe.

In Paraguay, the fugitives merged into Mennonite,
German speaking, communities. These were mainly
peaceful enclaves founded by 19th Century German
Protestants. They kept themselves apart, adhering to
their old Biblical beliefs. Some were ripe for takeover
by ruthless Nazis. The Paraguayans seldom ventured

into their territories. Since the Nazis came, fewer still returned.

In Phil's village, the regime was starkly authoritarian. Local landlords bought the allegiance of the small police force in Dr. Pedro P. Peña. They did pretty much as they pleased. Some were rumored to keep slaves from among the Guaycuru Indian tribes. He even heard tales that the Nazis hunted them for sport, from horseback, with packs of man-killer German Shepherds and vicious Dobermans.

Phil was disturbed by what he heard. Like all children, he had vivid nightmares ending in sticky, trembling fear. He remembered the nights when he jerked awake in the sweltering darkness, dripping with perspiration. In this recurring dream, ferocious men with rifles chased him, astride huge wild-eyed horses. Thrashing hooves tried to beat him to the ground as the horses reared up in front of him. Maddened and rabid red-eyed dogs snapped at him, with bloody fangs and slavering jaws.

Mostly though, his family life was happy. He loved to watch his mother preparing his favorite Sopa Paraguaya. Rather than being a soup, as its name implied, this was a delicious smelling dish made with onions, whipped pork fat, eggs and crumbled cheese, baked in the oven. He delighted in convivial gatherings of family and friends. They shared this dish and barbe-cued meat over an open fire pit.

Then everything changed for Phil. Like all Latinas, his mother was close to her family. One of her sisters, his aunt 'Tia Juanita', was a dark eyed beauty of 14, just a couple of years older than he. She was always laughing. He liked her, but alone among the village boys, did not find that she stirred his male hormones.

The local muchachos were always hanging around Juanita, but she was shy and kept them at a distance. She often walked to Phil's home after Sunday Services to play checkers with him. He was teaching her chess too.

That fateful day, his parents were visiting the house of a dying man, to give comfort and the last rites. Phil was winning their chess game. Then, Juanita glanced up at the open window. There was no glass and the shutters were fastened back. She gasped with surprise.

Horst, the blond, blue eyed son of the local landlord, was leering at them through the window. He was 19 and well-muscled. One of his cronies, Pedro, with the scarred face and permanent sneer, was with him. They sounded drunk, "Hey, Juanita! Why not come out and play with us?"

Eyes wide with fear she shook her head. They simply barged in through the unlocked door. Phil stood up to protest, but Horst whacked him hard with the side of an old Colt revolver that he was waving.

When Phil regained consciousness, he felt blood trickling down the side of his head, where a lump was growing. His arms and shoulders were pinned to the dirt floor by Pedro, whose heavy weight sat on his chest making him gasp for breath. Pedro's knees pressed Phil's shoulders to the floor, immobilizing his arms.

Phil struggled to get more air. He could hear muffled screams. Wrenching his head to the side, he saw Horst, pants down, grunting and thrusting into Juanita. He had a hand over her mouth. She wailed and struggled. Holding both her arms with one hand, he slapped her hard across the face. She gasped a prayer. "Mama Santa Maria save me!"

He hit her again, this time with his fist. "Stop fighting, you dirty little piece of trash. You're lucky to get this from me! Maybe you will have a German bastard, if you're lucky."

Her dress was torn down to her waist. Phil glimpsed her small breasts, almost white. They contrasted with her café au lait arms, shoulders, face and her dark brown nipples. He strained to move, but couldn't. He saw the frighteningly feral look in Pedro's eyes. He felt utterly helpless. Pedro socked him hard with his fist and grunted, "Hurry up, Horst! It's my turn next."

Horst gave another hard slap to the whimpering girl, then fastened his belt and knocked Phil out with another blow from the side of his revolver.

Juanita never spoke again after the rape. She seemed to be in constant trembling fear. She always refused to look at Phil, who had witnessed her degradation. For his part, he felt deep shame, self-loathing and guilt at failing to save his young aunt. His dreams were replaced with a new nightmare. When he woke, he boiled with helpless fury. He despised himself.

Phil was spitting angry vows of revenge. No one in the village could do anything. The local policía were in the pocket of the landowners. His father shipped him off to school in England, out of harm's way for fear of what he might do or say.

* * *

At his private school in England, which curiously the Brits called a 'public school', he disliked the harsh and unaccustomed discipline. The attitudes of the snooty and mostly wealthy pupils totally alienated him.

He sought solace in prayer. Unsurprisingly, he was top of the form in divinity. The other boys mocked his piety. "Hey, holy boy, go boil your head."

He really hated the place. That was until he realized that he was gay. His favorite teacher fondled him in a wood during a cross country run. He was excited and thrilled by the experience. Soon, he found like-minded boys in his house. He became rampantly and happily promiscuous.

He tried to tell his new friends about what was happening in Paraguay. He had learned much more since leaving the place. "Stroessner gets arms and military training from the CIA. He supports everything they do in Vietnam. He's totally corrupt. His chief torturer and head of the secret police, Pastor Coronel, keeps his victims in a bath of shit. Then he inserts electric cattle prods into their arses!"

"I say, you chaps! Red Saunders is babbling on about Paraguay again. Run for cover!"

It was a waste of his time. He learned to quietly nurse his anger and hatred. The God he prayed to, never answered him. He became an atheist.

Phil easily earned the grades to get into a politics course in the School of Latin American Studies at Essex. He and his close school friend Bill enrolled together.

***

At the Freshers' event, Phil felt strongly attracted to the Che-like character. Sadly, he turned out to be straight.

Phil's street cred from Latin America and being half Paraguayan gained him ready acceptance into the swing of things. His utter contempt for his private education and his obvious seething fury won him a place among the extremists in the School of Latin American Studies. Curiously several had wealthy backgrounds. They were in rebellion against their parents.

Being gay was also seen as an anti-establishment status symbol and therefore admired by Essex students. The Sexual Offences Act had only just been passed in 1967. It only tolerated sex acts between men over twenty-one.

Phil felt the most at home since he had left Paraguay. That night he managed to squeeze into his two and a half foot wide bed with Bill, his friend from school. After their usual frenzied and still illegal copulation, he dreamt happily of bloody revenge.

His Fresher's Day had been entirely satisfactory. Maybe from here he could change the world for the better. He never wanted to be helpless again. He was going to like it here.

CHAPTER 4
1968 LONDON AND PARIS-
THE YEAR OF LOST DREAMS

"I think the thing to do is to get a travel-ing yippee guerrilla theater band roaring through college campuses burning books, burning degrees and exams, burning school records, busting up classrooms."

John 'Tito' Gerassi, academic and author of *The Great Fear in Latin America*, survivor of a CIA attempt to poison a meal that he was sharing with Fidel Castro.

Three ranks of British bobbies, in their traditional tall helmets with shiny badges and dark blue uni-forms, linked arms. They blocked the road leading into Grosvenor Square Gardens and the looming grey bulk of the US Embassy. Facing them was a roaring mass of angry students and workers. They waved an angry sea of red banners and placards. Some hurled stones, bottles and other missiles.

Led by a lank-haired American with an electronic megaphone, the crowd rhythmically chanted over and over "Ho, Ho, Ho Chi Minh, we will fight and we will win!"

A red banner with black lettering 'Essex RSSF', Revolutionary Socialist Students Federation, was borne high over an especially aggressive group on the march. Mike could see his friends, Jerry, happy as usual; Phil Saunders, face contorted with fury and Sheila Reynolds, ruddy cheeked and screaming like a harpy. They shouted abuse and shook their fists and placards at the police lines. "Fascist bastards!" "Dirty pigs." "Why defend the CIA baby killers?"

The friends had agreed their plans the day before. Mike would march separately, under the red and black banners of the anarchists. Indeed, he felt more at home with the muscular Irish builders, militant car workers from the Ford plant at Dagenham and belligerent printers from Fleet Street. His friends felt that his northern accent would make him more accepted into this group than any of them. They all wanted to understand the militant workers. According to

Marxist theory, they would be essential to future revolutionary action. Mike also had a special mission.

A burly cop faced Mike. His eyes glared hatred. He bellowed, waving his truncheon, "OK, sunshine, come and get some!"

The massed crush of protesters in the confined street pulsed with energy derived from the rhythm of the slogans. Mike felt himself thrust forward by the crowd's curious hopping surge. The mob was like a huge and powerful snake, its bulk pushing its head, the front rank of protestors, into the police lines. The cops lashed down with truncheons. Girls were screaming. Split heads spurted blood.

Some of the more determined anarchists dismantled nearby scaffolding. They used the steel poles to break the police line. Mike smashed a fist into the fleshy cop's face, feeling a satisfying crunch. He karate-blocked a truncheon blow with his arm. A jolt of pain shot through the nerves of his forearm like an electric shock, but he felt no break. Then, he was spun round and somehow found himself whirled backwards, to be swallowed into the body of the marchers, away from the police lines. This was not in the plan. He struggled against the human tide, to get back to the front.

It seemed that those at the back pushed forward. Those at the fore, facing the rain of heavy truncheon blows, tried to get to the back. The result was the circulatory movement, temporarily sucking Mike away from the front rank. He pushed and shoved his way forward.

Finally, the cordon broke and over a hundred thousand furious marchers surged into Grosvenor Square. There, stood the awesome concrete mass of the US Embassy. An enormous bronze eagle with its wings spread was mounted high over the entrance, near its flat roof. Police cordons and mounted police deployed in defensive ranks in front of the broad steps to the doorway and the adjacent security fence.

There was a pause, as both sides eyed each other. Things were getting serious. The marchers could smell victory. If only they could breech this last line of defense. Equally battered and bruised and with their anger up, the police wanted revenge.

The protestors debouched into the square's gardens, behind low metal railings, trampling the daffodils. Another man with a megaphone started more chanting. "Hey! Hey! LBJ, How many kids did you kill today?"

This was interspersed with. "President Johnson... we want you... DEAD!"

The mob took up the chants and surged at the police lines. Mike thrust his way back into the front rank. He still had a job to do.

The crowd moved en masse to attack the embassy. The low metal fences around the square's gardens were bent, broken and trampled. Some marchers fell over them and were injured under the feet of others.

Suddenly, the huge horses of the mounted police charged into the crowd in a wedge. Their riders struck down at the protestors' heads with long riot sticks, left and then right. The muscled flanks of the horses shoved others to the ground. Mike could smell the sweating chestnut horse as it loomed over him. He glimpsed an anarchist hurling a metal dart from a pub dartboard into the horse's rump with his full strength. The poor beast reared up, eyes bulging and nostrils flaring. A bearded steel worker jammed a stout pole from a torn banner into the rider's stomach. It lifted him high out of his saddle. He crashed to the grass next to Mike, winded.

The police and the crowd battled for control of his struggling body. Mike threw himself at the police line and received a whack across the forehead for his pains. Next thing he knew, he was lifted bodily off his feet. The police line opened up to swallow him. He felt a rain of heavy blows as he was seized and carried behind the police line. His arms pinioned and help-less, he felt a strong hand groping for his testicles, squeezing hard. Pain lanced through his brain. As he passed out, he knew that he had achieved the first part of his mission. The next part would be trickier.

* * *

That May, on the bus to Paris after a stormy channel crossing on the ferry, Mike was discussing John Ger-rasi's book, *The Great Fear in Latin America* with his new girlfriend. Sarah was from Halifax in Yorkshire, conveniently only a few miles from his hometown of Todmorden.

* * *

A month earlier, from a payphone box in a pub off campus, he dialed the number he had been instructed to call each week. The usual male and slightly nasal voice of his control answered. As always, his heart beat faster and the hand holding the shiny and heavy black plastic phone started to sweat, as he listened. "There's someone we are very interested in. Go to the student notice board. Accept the lift offered by Sarah from Halifax, in exchange for help with money for petrol. Find out what you can. Report back next week at the same time." Without waiting for any com-ment or reply, the sinister voice clicked off.

* * *

Ready to return to Essex to start the new term, Mike waited nervously near Halifax bus station, wondering what to expect. Five minutes late, a rust-pocked and battered pale green Ford Cortina pulled up at the curb. The young female driver swung open the passenger door. Dumping his rucksack on the back seat, he jumped in.

They looked at each another appraisingly. He stared a little, finding her incredibly attractive. She had curly brown hair, dark brown eyes and a nose, which looked as though it had been slightly broken at some point. He thought it was cute. She was a bit skinny, but somehow she exuded a vibrant sexuality, strength and intelligence. Sarah broke the spell as she pulled away from the curb. She laughed at his staring, smiling with her full lips. "So, we have a few hours on the road. Tell me about yourself."

He shared his background and increasingly extreme political views. She seemed really interested, nodding from time to time and asking questions.

She told him that she was Jewish. She spoke with passion, eyes flashing, "My aunts, uncles and grandparents were all rounded up in Austria. They died during the Holocaust. Those Nazi bastards treated them worse than cattle being slaughtered."

"Dad and Mum managed to get to England in 1934, before the worst of it. They were penniless. Many of the English despised the Jews. My people had a hard time. You can understand why a socialist future with equality for all is so important to me. That's why I'm determined to fight against injustice. It seems that we have some ideals in common."

Mike felt that the hardships his own friends and family had suffered seemed suddenly very minor.

* * *

A few weeks later, and now passionate lovers, they were on a coach to Paris. Mike opined, "Gerassi knows what he's talking about regarding the fascists in Paraguay, led by Stroesner and about others in Bolivia and Argentina. Trujillo in the Dominican Republic ran the place like his own private brothel, raping anyone's wife he wanted. You should talk to my friend, Phil about Paraguay. He lived there until quite recently."

"That's all very well, Mike, but we need to fight here, not in Latin America. Maybe there are lessons to learn, but we must attack the seat of power right here in Europe. Che tried to take the struggle to Africa. He was murdered in Bolivia, and for what?"

Mike laughed, full of bravado. "You're right, Sarah. Let's see if we can kick out De Gaul this week and then we'll attack in the UK. The week after that we'll free the world!"

Her bright eyes looked excitedly at him and she gave him a hug. He loved her crinkly hair and sultry sexuality. He had met many Jews at Essex, including his buddy Jerry, who was on the coach a few seats behind, drinking himself happily into a stupor with the contents of a 7-pint party tin of best bitter.

All the Jews he had met at Essex were argumentative and mostly left wing. David Triesman, a leader of a student strike and a militant activist, was also Jewish. Sarah had told him, "Jews were well represented on the left and in most modern revolutions. This is partly because they suffered discrimination and vicious pogroms.

"Also, we are raised with a strong sense of moral justice. Our way of studying the Torah is to vigorously argue its meaning. This makes many of us articulately disputatious. Besides, the memories of the holocaust unite us all and make us combative. Never again!"

Mike wondered if all Jewish girls were as wild in bed as Sarah. She was insatiable. Bedding her was part of the plan, but the part he liked best. Increasingly, he felt bad about it. She was a good and lovely person and he was using her.

* * *

Jerry, Sarah and Mike sheltered in a Paris doorway, their eyes red, stinging and streaming from tear gas. The French riot police, the CRS, made the British bobbies look like pussy cats. They wore dark colored combat helmets and protective padding. Charging with their round riot shields they smashed as many skulls as they could.

The mob hurled petrol bombs at a group of flics off to the right. The petrol filled bottles arced overhead, trailing a small plume of fire from burning rags. Gasoline splashed across the cobbles where the cops stood. It flared up explosively as the rags lit the fuel when the bottles smashed.

The cops leapt back. Some beat out the fires from their comrades' burning uniforms. One or two rolled on the ground, their clothes ablaze.

The CRS charged back, retaliating with salvoes of rubber bullets. These 'baton rounds' were meant to be bounced off the ground, but a cop fired one right into Jerry's face from less than five yards away. Jerry slumped down a doorjamb. Blood gushed from where his nose used to be. Sarah screamed with anger. She went for the cop with a broken stave from a banner, sticking the splintered sharp end into his neck behind the ear. He too collapsed down screaming, trying to staunch the blood with a thickly gauntleted hand.

Mike grabbed her shouting, "There are too many of them. We have to pull back." He tried to pull Jerry by his collar, but he was like a sack of potatoes. Releasing Sarah, he felt for a pulse in Jerry's neck with his other hand. There was none. Their happy joking friend was dead. They abandoned him in the doorway and ran. They were chased by furious, stick wielding cops spilling from the back of a black van like a swarm of angry bees.

Mike dragged Sarah, struggling against him, round a corner. He saw a red daubed sign painted on the peeling white stucco of a wall. *"Soyez réalistes, demandez l'impossible."* Be realistic, demand the impossible.

* * *

That night, they sat at a table in a Latin Quarter bar, nursing their bruises and mourning. Head down, Mike was drowning his shock and horror at the death of Jerry with rough red wine. Sarah tried to comfort him with an arm around his shoulder. Both had tears in their eyes.

About twenty cops burst into the bar, seizing the patrons at random. The flics whacked them both on the head. They dumped them onto the cold metal floor of a dark blue Citroen van like sides of beef. As it drove off, they were jolted against the corrugated metal sides.

At the police station, Sarah was hauled off kicking and screaming. "Get your filthy hands off me you mother fucking fascist pigs!"

Mike wondered, *'Where did she learn her French? It certainly wasn't in the classroom!'*

Three cops lugged Mike, his arms handcuffed behind him, into an interrogation room. They threw him to the concrete floor. Then they gave him a thorough roughing up with their boots and fists.

He kept repeating, through broken and bleeding lips in schoolboy French, "Please call this number. It will help you."

Eventually, a sergeant passed this on to his superiors. Mike was left to stew, bruised and bleeding. He ached all over and slumped in a chair. An hour later, a harassed inspector bustled into the room. He addressed him brusquely in heavily accented English. "So, you are on our side. Our embassy in London confirmed it. We are to let you go."

"Yes, but I need to get Sarah Cohen out too. She's part of the group I am trying to infiltrate, 'the Angry Brigade.'"

"OK, we'll try to find out where she is. We are not interested in English revolutionaries. We have plenty of our own. If we have her, you are welcome. We have hundreds of rioters in custody. De Gaulle has the tanks moving in to protect the City. It will be a close run affaire, but if we need to, we'll grind the commies under the tank tracks."

* * *

While he waited for the French cops to find Sarah, Mike reflected on how he came to this point in his life. He remembered the big row he had with his closest friends and fellow agitators, Phil Saunders and Sheila Reynolds in her flat a few months earlier.

He had never met an openly gay person before and found Phil strange, but a staunch and reliable fellow socialist. He never fully described his experiences in Paraguay. Whatever they were, they had made him an extremist, even amongst the far left Essex militants.

Sheila was the strongest woman he had ever met. She often smoked a cigar and drank a glass or two of brandy, when not in public. She liked the good things in life and seemed well able to afford them. She was merciless in arguments, shouting down all opposition in a mockingly braying voice. It dripped with sarcasm, venom and superior intellect. She and Mike maintained their affair for a while. She still looked to him whenever her sexual needs drove her. Being a normal male he was only too happy to oblige. He liked her, despite her middle class affectations. In bed, she called him her 'bit of rough'.

Mike's dead friend Jerry had never been part of this inner circle. He was too jocular and was always laughing. He drank far too much to be trusted to keep his mouth shut. Mike was becoming increasingly sober to avoid the same problem.

As they planned, Mike rounded on Phil. "Look, I see the logic of trying to infiltrate the other side, but it's bloody dangerous."

"Don't look at me like that Phil. I'm not thinking of myself. Sure, we can discover stuff from them, but they'd watch me too closely for me to be useful. What if I gave something away inadvertently?"

Sheila laughed, rubbing her leg suggestively against him. "Then we should have to liquidate you my love. That'd be a great pity."

After further protest, he finally capitulated. His mission was to allow himself to be turned, after some resistance. Then to find out what they knew, he would further serve the revolutionary cause by trailing false scents and providing credible misinformation. He felt very uncomfortable with one of Phil's proposals, "Mike, you'll need to feed them minor players from our side from time to time."

"No way, Phil! Look, betraying comrades is something else. I just won't fucking do it!"

Phil gave him a hard stare. "Not all comrades are committed. Some see revolution as teenage fun. They'll go back to daddy and mummy and join the capitalist establishment. They aren't true comrades. They're dangerous dilettantes. They bring disrespect to the cause. As soon as they can, they'll be working as bankers, accountants, and lawyers and for big corporations. They *will* betray us!"

"Others act in ways which'll damage the cause rather than take us to victory. We have to harden our hearts and be ruthless. Remember our ultimate aims! Remember Che!"

* * *

Following his arrest in Grosvenor Square, Mike was proudly fed upwards by a detective sergeant. The sergeant had given him a good thumping in the cells. He congratulated himself on breaking the over-privileged young bastard.

Mike recalled the subsequent interview with Commander Glaster of the Special Branch. It was a tricky meeting. "Look, I know some really crazy people at Essex University. I'm actually a Labour Party supporter. If you let me go, I can keep you up to date on what's happening."

Glaster, a hard-bitten fellow Northerner, looked sceptical, "Just like that, eh? What about yer socialist principles, lad? Why should we believe anything you say?"

"OK, Mr Glaster, please let's try it for a couple of weeks and see what I turn up. You can still charge me after that, if you want to. There are some really dangerous people at Essex. I'll be risking my life, but it's the right thing to do. Look, I only came to demonstrate peacefully. I'm horrified by the violence."

Glaster had no informers at Essex. He was in touch with an ex-cop in the university security department, but he turned up little. The ever helpful, but miniscule Conservative student group was frightened and of no use at all. Its four members were well known and excluded from any really helpful information. Glaster needed results. University buildings had been burned and cars torched. He'd heard rumors of bombs. God knew what these lunatics would do next. Maybe Mike really could be useful. It was worth a risk.

* * *

In Paris, Sarah and Mike were reunited as two cops threw them down the steps of the police station, one after the other. Sarah, defiant to the last yelled. "Get your hands off my tits, you filthy pervert!"

One gave Mike a boot in the backside as a parting gift. As they limped away, Sarah looked at his heavily beaten and dirty face. She laughed, as she saw his concern at her own injuries. "Come on, a few bruises won't stop us. We'll make these fascists pigs pay! Let's get back on the streets!"

* * *

So 1968 ended. The French Government survived. The war in Vietnam fostered ever more atrocities: hardship and death for the poor peasants in the rice paddies.

Ever nastier weapons were deployed. They included bombs that spewed flechettes. These hardened plastic darts embedded themselves deep in human flesh. They were undetectable by X-rays and hampered surgery and recovery. Agent Orange sprayed from large aircraft defoliated enormous stretches of jungle with toxic chemicals, poisoning the earth far into the future.

Millions of anti-personnel mines were strewn indiscriminately. They could stay deadly for tens of years after any fighting was over. They would remain to maim and kill the farmers and future generations of children, playing or working in the fields.

GIs, on active service, most of whom had no idea what they were fighting for, became increasingly demoralized and scared. Those returning home, many of them horribly wounded, were yelled at and ostracized like war criminals or lepers. Some became street people. Others joined the protestors. Mostly, the elites wangled exemption or safe billets for their kids. George W. Bush arranged and enjoyed a safe haven in the Air National Guard. Bill Clinton and many others found reasons not to serve.

The media carried horrific images into homes in America and around the World. Buddhist priests stoically immolated themselves in protest. They sat cross-legged as flames engulfed their bodies. As an arm collapsed amidst flames, one monk repeatedly righted himself to his meditative posture.

Children were shown in press photographs, naked and screaming, seared by cloying napalm. A general executed a prisoner by blowing his brains out of the side of his head for the cameras. They recorded every gory detail for television and the newspapers. The horror of these things, brought into the living rooms of every household, cost the Americans the war.

* * *

Mike and his comrades met irregularly, in great secret, taking precautions not to be followed or overheard. Naturally, Sheila always chaired the meetings. It reduced her raucous interruptions of the others.

At one such meeting in December 1968 Sheila harangued them. "We've been kids playing at revolution. It was a stupid dream that we could achieve anything this year. Most of the other comrades are useless. Others are positively dangerous to our cause."

Mike said, "I agree; we need to play a long game. I'll burrow deeper into the confidence of the Special Branch. I've been introduced to some others, probably from MI5."

They agreed that Phil and Sheila would seek different entry points into the establishment, working to destroy it from within, even if it took a few years. Phil would pretend to regain his religion and use his connections to rise in the Anglican Church. Sheila would become active in the Labour Party, where she knew many senior figures and her parents' paper would buy her influence. They would all work to destroy the government, once they were deeply embedded.

Phil still looked worried, "I'm impatient for success. There's great danger here. If we keep putting off revolution, it'll never happen. We'll be seduced by the system. Let's all swear to meet at least once a year and never to give up on our drive to overthrow the fascist establishment."

The three of them clasped their right hands, looking each other in the eyes. Following Phil's lead, Mike and Sheila solemnly repeated, "I so swear!"

CHAPTER 5
THE CHAMPAGNE SOCIALIST

"No member of the commonwealth can have a hereditary privilege as against his fellow-subjects; and no-one can hand down to his descendants the privileges attached to the rank he occupies in the commonwealth, nor act as if he were qualified as a ruler by birth and forcibly prevent others from reaching the higher levels of the hierarchy through their own merit."

Immanuel Kant

Before moving to Essex, Sheila Reynolds had harbored serious doubts about the place. She had enjoyed her undergraduate days among the dreaming spires of Oxford University. Its glittering elite students were more like her. She loved the wild parties.

She mixed with and often slept with likely future government ministers, potential captains of industry, judges, top scientists and other potential winners. Even at twenty-one, they were all so confident of their places in the ruling elite. They saw their paths mapped out for them as bankers, stockbrokers or members of parliament. A scattering expected to succeed to peerages and seats in the House of Lords. Family contacts and wealth underpinned their expectations and natural sense of entitlement.

Sheila liked to seduce winners. It was not difficult to pick them out at Oxford. Some already flaunted pots of money on expensive lifestyles. There was always the best champagne at every party. One lover was president of the Oxford University Students' Union, a sure path to the top in politics. Others were stars of the debating society, sports blues and leaders of political clubs.

* * *

In 1967, Sheila was in the second year of her sociology doctorate at Essex. Her background had been privileged from the start, but socialist privileged. Her grandfather was a Labour Party member of parliament in 1924. The first Labour Prime Minister,

Ramsay MacDonald, led the government then. Her mother was an Oxford-educated trade union activist.

Her father, also a lifelong Labour Party member, owned a moderately left wing publishing house, founded by her grandfather. The profits from this gave the family a good standard of living, expensive education and access to the contacts and the corridors of power.

Sheila knew well that the working classes her party was supposed to represent often sneered at the likes of her. After her private schooling, she studied at her mother's alma mater in Oxford.

She chose Essex to complete her studies under Professor Peter Townsend, a family friend. He was a mild mannered and earnest man with graying hair, well respected in the left wing Fabian Society, a socialist think tank. He advanced both sociology and socialism through his studies of working class families in London's East End.

Townsend succeeded in persuading the UK's thinking classes to accept his idea of 'relative deprivation'. This raised the definition of poverty beyond the former metric of having enough to eat, some form of shelter, rudimentary education and emergency healthcare. He redefined poverty as relative to the wealth of others. In the fullness of time, one could be poor and still have a car, television sets and much else.

Sheila was a committed socialist, but she had chosen to stay away from Freshers' Day at Essex with its latest influx of undergraduate weirdoes. She wanted power and excitement. A route forward lay on the left. Despite her family's generations of involvement with the Labour movement, too little had been achieved to guarantee power. The landed aristocracy and the bloated plutocrats had survived every attempt to topple them. The country was still ruled by an elite. She would be part of it, but she did want more radical action. Her socialism was intellectual rather than derived from any personal hardship of her own. She had little empathy for common people but was good at faking it. She feigned a sense of fairness using her family background. She also had an urgent desire to be a leader and to make her mark. She was seeking like-minded people in this hotbed of dissent.

* * *

On Fresher's night, she sat up late in her digs and smoked a few joints with her radical friends. They discussed Regis Debray's new book, *Revolution in the Revolution*. Then a professor in Cuba, Debray had been fighting with Che in Bolivia. As a result he was a hero to many thinking socialists.

At three in the morning, she turned in, promising herself that she would miss her tutorial scheduled for 10am the next day. She just wished she could find a real man. Most of her men friends were wishy-washy and weak. She slept with them whenever she needed sex, but she felt there was something missing.

$$* * *$$

As the weeks after the Paris riots passed, Mike began to find his feet. He had chosen Essex partly because an economist that he admired was there. The Canadian Professor Richard Lipsey was the head of the Economics Department. Mike had studied Lipsey's textbook for his school examinations. Mike liked the course and did well, despite missing many lectures. His early absences were due to dope and alcohol-fueled late night discussions with those sharing the apartment. These ranged from consideration of Lautréamont's *Les Chants de Maldaror* to surrealism and extremist, left wing politics. Later he spent more sober days planning with Sheila and other comrades.

A huge amplifier and speakers blasted out music by Velvet Underground, the Nice, Traffic, Country Joe and the Fish and the Doors. It drowned out conversation. Use of an oil bubble machine projected onto the ceiling of the kitchen/dining area added light, if not enlightenment. The many colored oil bubbles pulsated and morphed into new shapes to the throb of the base. The amplifiers were so powerful that in daytime the music could be clearly heard at a bus stop, two miles away, on the bypass outside the campus.

* * *

Meanwhile, the tabloid press and the Times titillated their readers by reporting how Essex University was descending into a hotbed of sex and drug fueled anarchy. Three students were excluded from the University for being disruptive. They were refused any hearing and the charges were kept secret.

Students occupied key university buildings in protest at this Kafkaesque injustice paralyzing the place. There were marches against the Vietnam War in the nearby garrison town of Colchester.

Mike was amazed to hear one of the sociology lecturers provoking a hostile crowd of spectators on the route. "Remember you're all paying for us to get our education. This demonstration is at your expense!"

He moved on swiftly before a local taxi driver could land a blow. Mike challenged the lecturer. "Why are you trying to upset the working class? We need them on our side."

"We need to stir them up to fight against privilege. We are privileged. They need to hate us with real fury, so they can be turned against the elites in general."

The students consoled themselves that those in the working class who disagreed with socialism had been brainwashed. They were suffering from 'false consciousness.'

The handful of Conservative students fueled the press frenzy by inviting right wing cabinet Minister Enoch Powell to speak at the University. Powell had made an inflammatory anti-immigration speech not long before, speaking of the advent of 'Rivers of Blood.' This caused a near riot and resulted in further censorious press comment. Notoriety only encouraged increased student action and excitement, as the young people reveled in the public attention.

The student magazine published cruel caricatures by the student cartoonist Tom. One depicted the Duke of Edinburgh about to mount the Queen. His erection sported a tattoo 'by appointment to Her Majesty.' A union flag flew from its shaft. Allegedly, the Duke was shown the cartoon and was not amused. The police Special Branch started to take a deep interest in Essex.

***

Students returning from weekends in London stole cars to make the journey. The cars' stripped body shells were dumped beneath the back of the tower blocks and plundered of every useable part.

Mindless violence broke out. There were rapes, razor slashings and stabbings. Mike remembered again that this was how rats behaved when kept in high-density confinement.

Mike's Flat 14 in Raleigh Tower was far from immune to all this. A chemistry student supplied large quantities of absolute lab alcohol. This added power to the fruit punch and fueled many wild parties, together with gallons of home brewed beer and hallucinogens.

One night Mike and the other denizens of Flat 14 were flying high on LSD. Someone set fire to a plastic dining chair, using sugar to fuel the flames. Toxic smoke soon blackened the walls and started to descend from the ceiling. The trippers were forced to crawl around the floor to avoid choking on smutty, noxious fumes.

One lad danced wildly round the room, scooping up and spilling burning PVC with a spoon. He threw flaming plastic on to foam cushions and the sofas.

Others raced on all fours round and round the central wall. Finally, someone started hurling burning furniture from the windows. Everyone joined in, watching the tumbling, burning chairs smack on to the pavement, fourteen floors below.

Eventually, when the fire was nearly out, the police and the fire brigade arrived, all sirens and flashing blue lights. A student rushed out of the darkness and tossed a large lump of concrete at the lead car. It bounced off the hood and crashed through its windscreen. The driver reversed back at speed, smashing into the one behind.

Cops jumped from their vehicles like a shoal of frenzied piranhas, but swiftly scrambled back in, as a refrigerator narrowly missed them, tumbling down from high in another tower and thumping into the roadway with a loud bang. The police inspector in charge ordered the convoy to withdraw, in order to avoid injury to the firemen and his constables.

The university's official enquiry into the incident stated, *"A discarded cigarette caused the fire.... The student residents bravely tried to extinguish the flames. They prevented the fire spreading to the rest of the tower by throwing the burning furniture from the windows."*

The last thing the university authorities needed was more bad publicity.

The police never openly showed themselves on campus again. Their covert surveillance was heightened. They desperately wanted to avenge their humiliation.

* * *

Following the excitement of the fire in Raleigh 14, Sheila, Phil and Mike were talking in Phil's student lodgings. Sheila was furious. "You stupid prat, Mike! How can we foment a revolution if you are known for being involved in drug and drink fuelled arson? That was a narrow escape. Tell him, Phil!"

"She's right, Mike. We can't work together, if you put drugs and drink before the cause. Who knows what you might give away, if you were on a trip or stoned out of your mind?"

"Look, I'm sorry you two. I'll not do it again. I'll show you I'm serious. Let's discuss the Angry Brigade."

Neither Sheila nor Phil had heard of the Angry Brigade, until Mike was targeted on Sarah and her co-conspirators, by Commander Glaster. Mike remembered the group discussion after his trip to Paris in 1968.

"Look, I think I love Sarah. Just because she's kept the Angry Brigade to herself and hasn't invited me in doesn't mean we should sell them out to Glaster. They're really committed. I found a fully loaded Sten gun, hidden in their London apartment, along with a cache of gelignite. From what little we know, they seem to be a tight cell modeled on the Baader-Meinhof Red Army Faction. We want action and they're ready to take it. We're sat on our backsides talking and they are doing things!"

Phil took a hard line, "Come off it, Mike. Baader, Meinhof and the rest are just over-privileged German middle class kids. They go round bombing things and kidnapping people. What have they actually achieved? The Angry Brigade let off dainty little bombs. They've done little damage so far."

He brightened up, "You said she has a submachine gun. Later, we'll need every weapon we can get. See if you can pinch it, when you get a chance."

Mike balled his fists and looked daggers at Phil. Quickly Sheila weighed in on Phil's side. "Phil's right, Mike. If you give her up to Glaster, he'll be your friend for life. It's just what you need, to give you an extra boost up. Besides, if you are ever that desperate for a shag, you know where I am."

Mike winced at the last. Then he argued long and hard. Eventually, he reluctantly capitulated, partly due to pressure from Glaster, who seemed about to lift Sarah anyway.

Mike told Glaster everything he knew, including information about the Sten gun and the explosives. Glaster was delighted. A week later, the Angry Brigade was rounded up.

* * *

Mike lay in his bed weeping tears into an already wet pillow, his shoulders heaving. He regretted his betrayal and not having warned Sarah ever after. He never saw her again. He had begged Glaster to cut a deal with her. The only response was, "Don't be naïve son. She's a fucking terrorist bitch!"

Sarah and all the Angry Brigade members received long jail sentences. Defiant to the last, Sarah died in prison on hunger strike.

As he moved towards his retirement, Commander Glaster thought that he had put paid to left wing revolutionaries in the UK for good. He was wrong.

CHAPTER 6
SOLDIER, SAILOR...

*"Not believing in force is the same as not be-
lieving in gravity."*

Leon Trotsky

In 1975 Mike was now a sergeant in Britain's elite
and clandestine Special Air Service, the SAS. As he
lay hidden amongst some thorny bushes in central Africa, drenched with sweat and feasted on by
mosquitos, he felt he was earning his place in the establishment the hard way. His anxious face streaked
with green and black cam cream, he scanned the far
bank of the river with his binos. A large crocodile
with prominent plates on its back slithered from a
sandbar in the middle of the water, slipping under
the languidly flowing surface and disappeared without trace.

He briefly closed his eyes, considering how to get across the river and picturing their target village down-stream. For a map they only had an aerial photo-graph of the village taken months earlier from a gov-ernment transport plane, with a handheld camera. The definition was fuzzy and unhelpfully, parts of the photograph used to make the map had been ob-scured by clouds. He calculated that the village was downstream round the next bend in the river.

Mike's SAS instructors had learned to move slowly and quietly through the jungle from experience gained during the Malayan Emergency in the 1950s. They had overcome the Chinese backed Communists and learned valuable lessons in jungle warfare.

Mike silently gestured by putting the fingers of his right hand downwards on the top of his jungle hat. From their cover, the others in his five-man team re-sponded to the signal. They stealthily converged on his position. One spoke quietly, "What do you think, Mike?"

Mike briefed his team. "From the shots we heard earlier, the village is four clicks down-stream, on the other side of the river. It'd take us too long to hack through the jungle and cross there, so we'll need to float down on rafts. There are crocs, so we can't just swim over. We'll need to keep our arms and legs inboard. John and Larry, you will go and get the locals. For Christ's sake, keep 'em quiet."

John said, "We'll tell 'em we think there's a machine gun nest across from us. That should do it."

Mike continued, "Get 'em to cut three light rafts and bring 'em here. Tim and Will, go back a click so you won't be heard, and cut a smaller raft for the three of us. We three will float past the village after dark. We'll move in on the huts from downstream around first light. When we open fire, the rest of you and the main party will come in from upstream and attack. We'll set an exact time for the start when you get back here. Any questions? All right. Go!"

***

The village was unusually noisy. The rebel leader had taken possession of the chief's house. The chief would not be needing it any more. His headless body lay in the dusty street outside, already stinking, bloated and buzzing with flies. The leader and a couple of his men were drunkenly raping the chief's screaming wives and daughters amidst a pile of empty beer bottles looted from the village store. The store owner was left dead inside with a gaping exit wound in his chest. Next to him lay a small baby. Its brains had been dashed out against a wooden pillar.

A hundred yards inland, further up the only street, there were more screams and cruel laughter. The other fourteen rebels were drinking heavily. They were raping three nuns and the two handicapped girls that had not fled into the jungle when the first shots were fired.

* * *

A few hours later, just before dusk, the three other SAS men arrived back with the government troops and their rafts. Mike looked despairingly at one native soldier who laughed out loud. The colonel casually lopped his head off with a single swing of the razor edged panga, which he'd picked up when in exile in Kenya. The other local troops fell silent, rolling their eyes in terror.

Mike gritted his teeth to contain his anger at the pointless death. He spoke quietly in English to the colonel and his number two. The number two translated most of what he heard to the rest of the men. "OK, Sir, me and these two of my men will come in from downstream at 05:30 hours. You, Sir, will lead the main group into the village from upstream. You need to be in position by 05:15 and absolutely silent. When we open fire, you attack. Is that understood?"

The colonel snarled at him, "Remember, I'm in command here. We do it my way! You are just advisers!"

Mike sighed wearily. He had heard that many times before, "Sorry, 'Sir'. In that case, why don't you lead the attack and we'll stay here on this side of the river, to cover any retreat."

The colonel grunted. "No! Your men can go in first, from both directions. I will lead my men to support the attack from upstream. We will be the second wave and secure the victory."

Mike forced himself to smile, replying, "Good strategy. Sir! Please remind everyone that our mission is to take their leader alive. He has important information about the rebel forces."

* * *

Mike's small raft drifted slowly past the village. It floated just beneath the water's warm surface due to the weight of its load. The three SAS men were sodden. The red glow from the embers of a smoldering hut in the village gave a little light. Mike noted that the boats one might expect in a river community had gone. He hoped most of the villagers were safe and hiding somewhere in the surrounding rainforest. A dog started barking. The SAS men held their breath hoping no one would flash a torch on their raft. Mike clicked off the safety catch on his M16. Then from somewhere in the village there was the crack of a gun, a whimper and then total silence.

* * *

At 05:00 in his position just below the village, the hairs on Mike's neck stood up. He whipped round and saw the whites of Tim's eyes, just three yards away. He had returned from his recce of the village. '*Not bad, to get that close before I sensed him,*' thought Mike.

Tim whispered, "It's grim Mike! There are a few bodies, including a Mongol girl with her hands cut off. There are no guards posted. They seem to be in two buildings, a big one by the river and some kind of mission building just over there."

"OK, Tim, we'll go for the mission. Flash bangs through the windows and door. When we've identified the leader, we kill the rest. Let's hope the other team is ready. If not, we fight through and go for the other building. If the others make their attack, keep off the street. We don't want to go down from their wild shooting."

"OK, Skip."

✳ ✳ ✳

At exactly 05:30 the stun grenades went through the door and windows of the mission. The rebels inside, already befuddled from drink, were deafened and disoriented by the blasts. They had no time to go for their weapons. Mike's team heard other shots from down the street. They swiftly tied the hands of their captives behind their backs with plastic ties.

Then they saw another dead child about nine years old, ripped wide open around her genitals. Two partly clothed nuns lay dead nearby, their breasts hacked off. A third nun, a white woman, her tongue ripped out and both hands hacked off, was whimpering with fear in a corner.

Mike set his lips tight. "Check them for watches."

"Only one, Skip."

The nun looked pleadingly into Mike's eyes. In answer to her silent but obvious prayer, he shot her in the head. "Keep the one with the watch. Kill the rest!"

Mike and his team prodded their terrified remaining captive down the street in front of them. There was yelling and shouting around the chief's house. The government troops were wild with excitement, firing long bursts into the air from their Kalashnikovs.

Mike pushed past the joyous Africans and entered the charnel house. The colonel was peeling off strips of skin from a screaming rebel. The man was held down on a bloody table by two soldiers. The two SAS men in the colonel's team were being kept back at gun point by four of the colonel's men. Two others were ravishing a badly beaten young girl, the only one left from the chief's family.

Mike fired into the air. "Stop this!"

Everyone watched Mike and the colonel. Mike's team fingered their triggers.

"Who do you think you are? I command here." With that the Colonel blew the brains out of his captive to emphasize his point. It was the last thing he did.

Mike nearly cut him in two with a burst from his M16, rapidly switching his aim to the four who held their guns on his team. They were in shock and fell as Mike's whole team opened up on all those with weapons. The noise of gunshots in a confined space was deafening. Empty cases ejected from the sides of their guns fell like hail. Mike's captive groveled on the floor. In the sudden silence, Mike groaned, "Damn! The only useful prisoner is dead."

Mike had noted that the colonel was now wearing a Rolex, taken from the rebel leader. He turned and shot his prisoner with the inferior watch in the forehead.

"OK. We'll bring the girl. Finish off the rest and clean up. Then let's get out of here."

* * *

They paddled their rafts back across the river in silence. Mike looked back. He could see the burning buildings of the chief's house and the mission. He thought to himself, *'If only we could have saved the village, before all this happened. All this and no information.'*

Mike was taking his turn to carry the girl over his shoulder in a fireman's lift. He felt bonded to this scrap of life. When she died two hours later, he felt her go still. He gently laid her down and checked her pulse. They left her and pushed on through the jungle.

Mike felt as though his heart was crushed and vowed to himself, *'One day I'll come back here. If the surviving villagers return from the jungle, I'll help this village.'*

CHAPTER 7
SPREADING TENTACLES
THROUGHOUT THE
ESTABLISHMENT

Listen, Watch, Learn.

"Those who make peaceful revolution impossible will make violent revolution inevitable"

John F. Kennedy

In 1992 Mike Sheila and Phil were meeting in historic Gayhurst House in Buckinghamshire. The following is from the Website of the Gayhurst Historical Society.

"The manor of Gayhurst, then called Goathurst, was mentioned in 'The Doomsday Book.' The present structure was started in

the early XVI th Century. It was built of Northampton honey-colored sandstone. It has leaded windows in stone mullions. The pillars that support the front porch have graffiti marked 1644, when elements of Oliver Cromwell's rebel army marched through Gayhurst.

In 1605 Gayhurst was the home of a treasonous plotter, Sir Everard Digby. 'The Gunpowder Plot' of that year was a foiled attempt by 13 Catholic conspirators to blow up King James I of England, at the state opening of Parliament in Westminster Hall. He was also James VI of Scotland, which was a separate kingdom at that time. The plotters believed James had broken a promise to allow Catholics freedom of worship. They planned to enthrone a Catholic Princess in his place.

The plotters secreted barrels of gunpowder in the cellars of Parliament. The King's spymaster discovered the plot by intercepting secret letters. Guido Fawkes, the military leader of the plot, was captured in the cellars of parliament as he attempted to light the gunpowder. The other plotters were hunted down. Digby was captured in a wood, after trying to fulfill his mission. This was to raise rebellion in the

Midlands. He was tortured on the rack. After confessing and begging for clemency, he was hanged, drawn and quartered for his part in the treasonous plot.....

The main house is currently divided into private apartments, many with historic features. There are secret passages, tunnels leading away from the house and a priest hole in the building. The extensive surrounding parkland and lakes were laid out by Capability Brown in the 18th Century."

* * *

Unknown to the other current residents, one apartment was owned by an offshore trust, secretly controlled by the Right Honorable Sheila Reynolds. She was now a member of Parliament and the opposition Labour Party's strident Shadow Minister for Social Services. Most of the other residents were often away in their other properties or travelling abroad. A few discreet comings and goings would not be noticed here in the Buckinghamshire countryside.

In her apartment in this historic place, the new gunpowder plotters met. They were showing a few years since their days at Essex. Phil was going prematurely bald. Mike was tanned, tough and fit, but had lost an eye in the Falklands War. Sheila looked well groomed, but her smart clothes could not entirely mask a thickening waist and spreading haunches.

Their common and determined desire was to repeat the Gunpowder Plot, but with a different ending. Each enjoyed the vibes from the home of their illustrious predecessor. The 1640's association with the rebellion against King Charles I enhanced Mike's comfort with this place. Cromwell had been a revolutionary soldier like himself and had Charles I executed.

Each time they arrived at Gayhurst, they passed the large portrait of Digby in the main hall. He was dressed in a red velvet doublet with a white lace ruff and matching red hose. Reputedly he had been a darling of the court prior to his trial. His picture was a good reminder of the perils of getting caught and the need for absolute secrecy.

Sheila watched Phil pouring coffee for her and Mike. He smiled and announced proudly, "It's from South America of course. We grow the best coffee."

They had all dressed down for the meeting, so as not to attract undue attention on arrival. They came in modest hired cars for the same reason. Though Gayhurst Court's residents were rather quiet, it would not do to excite their curiosity.

Phil was not wearing his more colorful purple bishop's shirt. Sheila looked mischievously at his simple clerical collar. "Phil, do you never feel strange wearing that dog collar? After all, you're an atheist."

Phil smirked and winked at her, "Ha, I feel no stranger than you do pretending to be a Labour Party supporter when really you're a revolutionary socialist. What's the big difference? We all agreed to pursue separate careers within the establishment. As a back -in-the-closet gay, I relish the occasional opportunity to wear a long and colorful dress without attracting ribald comments."

Sheila's smile vanished. She became all business. "You're right, of course and never forget, we put you back in the closet. You'd never have become a bishop if we hadn't arranged all that."

She smugly clasped her hands over her increasingly portly stomach. "Let's face it: we're all doing pretty well in our different roles. Mike, our Falklands war hero, now runs a powerful and extremely well connected security business. Maybe we should add you to the list of those to be eliminated, Mike?"

As Mike smiled sardonically at her, she continued, "My lot will win power at the next election if that clown John Major carries on being such a pathetic prime minister. People are still angry with Margaret Thatcher, though I secretly admire her. They'll vote us in this time."

"You, my Lord Bishop, have a seat in the House of Lords, no less, and a crack at becoming the Archbishop of Canterbury very soon. Of course, I'll be putting a word in the right circles for you. Maybe Mike could post some pedophile pictures on your rivals' computers to mess up their chances?"

Mike retorted, "That's easily done, but there are more subtle ways that we can tilt the pitch in Phil's favor. We'll do it, too. He will be chosen, but not quite yet. Two of his rivals are women. It would be harder to pin pedophilia on them. Maybe coming out as gay for a second time might even help, Phil."

"Meantime, the more we build my firm's capabilities in cyber warfare and win contracts with the UK Defence Ministry, the more we need to realize that any electronic communications can easily be intercepted and accessed. Britain is already a police state. Most folk just don't know it yet. The intercepts, we now have access to, allow us to listen in to the rich and powerful, but we also need to be aware that our own conversations are vulnerable too."

Sheila fidgeted with her Pimms. Mike's computer warfare team had removed certain of her sexual indiscretions from the paper and electronic records, when the Conservative Party had planned to out her in the press. "Point taken, Mike, let us move back to Phil. Practicing Anglicans are a minority these days, but they do have influence, although they reckon only twenty percent of UK citizens claim to be Anglican, and only one percent attend regular services. There is a definite loyalty to that religion, especially among the staid middle classes, whom we might expect to be anti any attempt at revolution. I'm told there are seventy million Anglicans around the world. Being able to play the God and the morality cards is very important in times of crisis. People start to go back to the churches then. We do intend to create one hell of a crisis!"

Phil said, "You have no idea how embedded the Anglican Church is in UK society and culture. We have our bishops as legislators in the House of Lords. Most state schools start the day with our prayers. Many societies, hospitals and charities have strong Anglican connections. Being an Anglican bishop gives me an instant image of caring, reasonableness and being a good fellow. It can be a great asset in masking and even legitimizing subversion and radical action.'

Sheila enthusiastically took up Phil's refrain. "Our collective connections and your signal and surveillance intelligence, Mike, give us insights and admittance to important centers of influence. Between us we can access wealth, people and information. When the time comes to attack, we'll all be well placed. We'll have the resources and knowledge to make our revolution successful. Revolution from within is unexpected and harder to resist."

Mike retorted, "We'll be too bloody old, if we wait much longer!"

"Too right!" Phil echoed, thinking, '*Sheila spends so much time waffling in that mother of all talking shops, The House of Commons that she can't stop.*'

Sheila prattled on about various things that they had already agreed. Yet again, Mike felt pangs of guilt over his great act of betrayal. He often brooded in the night about Sarah. He had done a great wrong.

* * *

At a later meeting at Gayhurst House, the three of them walked over the sun drenched fields to a quiet, nearby nature reserve. It was August and the blackberries and elderberries were forming. The grasses and wildflowers were shoulder high in the still air and butterflies fluttered around the paths.

In a secluded shady glade, they enjoyed a picnic, which Mike had carried effortlessly in his pack. They discussed the state of the country and what it meant for their plans, over glasses of crisp white Vinho Verde.

Sheila opened the conversation. "Look, we've seen the world turned upside down in the last few years. The socialist model that we aspired to, based on some early success in the communist bloc, has failed utterly. Maybe it's good that we didn't have the chance to implement such a model. We've learned from experience."

Mike said, "We all thought that the miners, the power workers, the printers and the rest of the militant trade unions could bring down Margaret Thatcher's government. They lost. She faced them down. Then by privatizing and closing most of the coal industry she destroyed their power. We were wise to hold ourselves back at the last moment and to avoid involvement. We were too weak then and we still are."

"Given popular feeling in the UK, we did well to avoid possible links with the Provisional Irish Republican Army, the only extant armed opposition to government here."

Phil added, "Yes, it wouldn't have helped that you and your mates in the SAS were busy hunting some of them down in Northern Ireland and here in England too. Besides, allying with them would have turned most of the population on the mainland against us. But all this is fine. When are we actually going to do something?"

Resenting the further interruption, Mike gave Phil a pained look. Phil ignored it, remembering the rape of his aunt, his feelings of helplessness and his urgent need to act. He continued fiercely, "It's all well and good, but what have we actually done? Absolutely nothing is the answer! The Berlin wall came down, the Soviet Empire crumbled and we're still sitting around on our backsides. It's time to plan a different way forward. Remember the oath we three took in '68. I want to come out of this weekend with a plan and a timetable before we all die of old age."

* * *

Yet again he was disappointed. They merely agreed to meet again in a few months. Mike jogged to catch up with Phil at the back of the house, as he was leaving. Grabbing him by the sleeve of his jacket, he tried to assuage his concerns. "I've got some ideas. I promise to think them through and come with concrete proposals next time and soon."

"Rubbish," grunted Phil, jerking his arm away. He stomped off to his car. He shouted over his shoulder, "If anyone needs me, I'll be in Paraguay!"

Troubled, Mike loped back to the house. He managed to catch Sheila before she left, tapping on her car window. She opened the tinted glass. "We have a problem with Phil, Sheila. We always knew he was seething about Paraguay. I think he really means to go there this time. We have to stop him. Paraguay's a sideshow. We must keep him here!"

Sheila got out of her car and looked up at Mike. "How can we do that? Besides, it's not a sideshow to Phil. It's gnaws at his soul every minute of every day. Until it's resolved, he'll be unreliable. Maybe we should eliminate him."

"Whoa, no need to be nasty. You block him from going, Sheila. You have the contacts for that. I'll deal with his problem."

CHAPTER 8
A FAVOR FOR A COMRADE

"We should forgive our enemies, but not before they are hanged."

Heinrich Heine

Phil stood by his carry-on bag at London Heathrow Airport's Terminal 2, amongst other anxious passengers. He looked at the large departure board, clutching his tickets for the first leg of his flight to Paraguay. He had shed his clerical garb and was travelling inconspicuously in jeans and a bush jacket. He needed to appear as ordinary as possible.

It would soon be time to go through customs and passport control. He checked his boarding pass for the third time. It was in the name of Antonio Vargas. It matched his counterfeit passport.

The public address announcement made him look up "Iberia Airlines announces that flight 7447 to Madrid is delayed. Passengers please check at our airline desks for more information."

"Oh, hell!" muttered Phil. Then two large plain-clothes policemen flashed a warrant card in his face, and one simply said, "Please come with us, Mr. Vargas."

He thought of making a run for it, but where could he go?

* * *

Shlomo wrenched the gear lever of the dusty Toyota Land Cruiser into a lower gear, as it bounced along the sun baked, deeply rutted road, raising a small dust cloud. He gunned the engine and drove further away from the township of Dr. Pedro P. Peña in Paraguay. Turning his head, he spoke to his three teammates in Hebrew. "Those schmuck cops were a bit too careful checking our passports for my liking."

Avi, the team leader remarked, "Well, the twenty-dollar bill in my passport kept them off our backs. Always remember this, guys, a bribe should never be so big as to lead a greedy cop to thinking he can shake you down for more. Big bribes can create and elevate interest rather than deflecting it. Besides, why would they worry about a bunch of Chilean geologists? Our covers and permissions are all good."

The Mossad team had conducted similar missions in Chile and Argentina in recent years from their permanent base in Buenos Aries. They drove on with only the roar of their diesel engine breaking the silence. Then they pulled off the road, secreting their vehicle behind some bushes. Carefully, they camouflaged the car and brushed away any tire tracks. Offloading and shouldering their heavy packs and weapons, they hiked to the hacienda at a fast pace.

* * *

Horst Bauer sprawled in a leather easy chair. He was in the wood paneled office of his hacienda, savoring his third glass of a 12 year-old malt whisky and listening to his sound system. He was flushed with the drink as usual, beating out the rhythm of the German marching band with a fat cigar. It played his favorite Nazi march, 'Der Horst Wessel Lied'. The song was written in memory of his namesake. Horst Wessel was a member of the SA Brown Shirts and a minor Nazi thug. He had died in a street fight in 1930. The Nazi propaganda machine made him into a hero.

Pedro Gonzalez sat next to Bauer in a less comfortable chair set in front of a large glass display cabinet. Both men had aged badly and gone to fat, their faces blotched and wrinkled.

The cabinet contained part of Horst's gun collection. There was a standard German officer's 9mm Luger. A Mauser pistol, with its detachable stock in place, was displayed next to it. Horst generally sported the Walther PPK, his father's personal weapon. It was similar to that carried by the Führer himself. There was also a machine pistol MP40. All of these weapons were lovingly maintained and used regularly to hunt animals or the local native tribesmen. For hunting humans Horst liked the long barreled Mauser C96 pistol. Its 7.62mm ammunition made it effective up to 150 yards, due to its high muzzle velocity. He caressed it with his eyes through the glass.

A bust of Hitler stood on the leather top of the highly polished desk. The portrait of Horst's father, in a heroic pose and wearing his gray SS Standarten-führer's uniform, hung over the fireplace. The silver oak leaves of his rank gleamed on black patches either side of his collar. His stance proudly showed off the SD patch on his right forearm. This denoted membership of the feared Sicherheistdienst, the notorious Reich Security Department. The ironcross, first class hung from a chest pocket button. His peaked cap bore the silver death's head badge of the SS, below the embroidered Reich eagle. He was smiling.

The portrait was flanked by two Nazi standards. They were antiques from the first Nuremburg Rally. Each black staff was topped by a large gilded swastika in a metal circle. A gold-fringed pennant hung horizontally across each pole. The pennants were scarlet and each was dominated by its black swastika on a white circle.

A silver framed photograph of the proud Standartenführer, shaking hands with Hitler, also stood on the desk, opposite the bust. Horst was especially pleased that his father had served in department B of the SD. It was the group responsible for ethnic and racial matters. His father had died of cancer the year before. He often told Horst that he had personally liquidated over a thousand Jews, Gypsies and Slavs, some by strangling them with his bare hands. Naturally, countless others were killed on his orders. Horst loved to listen to such stories with adoring eyes.

He had inherited the Standartenführer's SS dagger, personally presented by Himmler. The razor sharp blade was etched in Gothic scripted German. 'My honor is my loyalty'. Horst frequently dwelt on the thought that the Reichführer SS, Heinrich Himmler himself, had held it in his own hand during the presentation ceremony. Now he owned the very same weapon, imbued with mystical power. He always carried it to meetings of the other Nazi families, on such special occasions as Hitler's Birthday. He relished the jealous looks of the other Nazis. His lineage gave him precedence in the tight knit community.

Oft times, he used the dagger as a letter opener. It was also perfect for slitting the throats of those he wanted to kill, usually while Pedro and a couple of other cronies held them still and helpless.

He puffed up his chest, "One day, Pedro, we Germans will raise the Reich from the ashes back to its former glory!"

* * *

The following is translated from 'La Estrella de Paraguay', an on-line news site.

> "Reports are coming in from the town of Dr. Pedro P. Peña in Chaco Province in the west. They say that there has been a massacre in an isolated Mennonite compound, outside the city. Over thirty men and six women are reported dead. Most had their hands fastened

behind their backs and had been dispatched with a shot to the head.

There was a series of explosions. These and prolonged gunfire were heard by people walking on a road two kilometers away. There are also reports of extensive fires burning into the hours of darkness.

Police are investigating. There are rumors that neo-Nazis attacked the community and are responsible. A special detective team from the capital, Asunción, will arrive tomorrow to take over the investigation.

The Mennonite community is a German-speaking group that keeps very much to itself. This village was founded in 1946. This is the first reported murder in the area."

* * *

Mordechai Farbstein, chief of the top secret Mossad assassination group Kidon, was in his office in Tel Aviv. He made a brief call on his secure line.

"Hi Mike, it's done."

"Did they get the pictures?"

"Yes, they did. You'll have them by tomorrow."

"Thanks, Mordechai, I owe you one."

"That's OK, Mike. It was a nasty nest of Nazi vipers. It had to be done."

"Bye, Mike."

Mike replaced the handset and sat for a moment, wondering how Phil would take the news.

* * *

Phil tried talking to those seizing him, as they forced a cloth bag over his head and bundled him into the waiting car. One of the detectives either side of him cut him off. "You are being held under the Prevention of Terrorism Act 2005. You were attempting to board an aircraft with a false passport. We aren't authorized to talk to you. You'll be questioned later."

Phil was stewing in a secure room somewhere near Heathrow airport. He knew roughly where he was, because the journey in the unmarked police car only took about 10 minutes. He could hear planes taking off overhead from the windowless room where he was confined.

He sat nervously, unhandcuffed on the bed, wondering whether their plans to take over the UK were discovered. His meals were pushed through the flap in the steel door, by an even more uncommunicative and forbidding guard.

On the sixth day, he was frog marched to an interview room by two silent and muscular men. They wore dark blue uniforms, without insignia. He sat down in one of the two chairs.

After a few moments, Mike breezed in, smiled at him and said, "Hi, Phil," taking the other chair. He put a laptop and a briefcase on the table between them.

Phil, glared at him, paused for a deep breath and demanded, "What the heck is going on, Mike?"

"We couldn't let you go charging off to Paraguay, Phil. It would've endangered everything."

Phil looked about to interrupt, but Mike held up a hand. "Just a minute, Phil, let me explain. We understood what needed to be done and we did it for you."

Phil gave him a pained look and spat out through gritted teeth, "Mike, I needed to do it myself."

Opening and switching on the laptop, Mike tapped a few keys and turned the screen to Phil. "Watch the video, Phil. It needed more than you to do it."

Phil gripped the sides of the table to control his temper. His knuckles showed white. The video panned across several properties in a large compound. It cut to the office with the bust of Hitler and the portrait of the Standartenführer. Phil saw his nemesis, Horst, tied to a chair, bloodied and blubbing from a severe beating. His nose was smashed.

In the background, a masked Shlomo was piling up the portraits and Nazi relics into a heap. He was affixing explosives to the pile. Horst spat out a few broken teeth. He stammered out a long confession in Spanish. It included the rape of Phil's aunt and at least thirty murders. Occasionally, as his voice trailed off into blubbing, his interrogator's hand appeared from off screen and gave him a shock with a Taser. This caused him to writhe and scream and then to continue.

Phil stared intently at the screen. The thickly accented Spanish of the interrogator asked, "What are you, Horst?"

Horst croaked back what they had beaten into him, "I'm a filthy Nazi swine and not fit to live."

"Before we kill you, you need to know that we always castrate rapists first." Horst cringed and whimpered in terror.

The camera then switched to another chair, where a broken Pedro, eyes wide with terror, received the same treatment. Patches of his hair had been torn out, leaving blood seeping from his skull. There followed a video clip of both their heads being jerked backwards by their hair. A single slash across each throat from the SS dagger resulted in the spraying of blood over the camera lens.

Phil let out a long shuddering sigh and slumped back in his chair. The rest of the film showed more bodies, burning buildings and explosions. Mike paused the video.

Phil sat silent for a while. Then he murmured softly, "Thanks, Mike."

Mike spoke gently, "There's more, Phil."

A further clip showed two graves, side by side in the mission churchyard. The simple wooden crosses bore the names of his aunt and his father. There was also a photograph of his mother, asleep in a hospital bed.

"We had her medivacked to Geneva. You can visit her there. She has angina and they've inserted a couple of stents. She wants to go back to Latin America. We'll send her after a few weeks, when she's rested."

"A car is waiting to take you wherever you want to go next. There are records to show that you just spent the last few days in a private clinic after a suspected pulmonary embolism. You'll be pleased to hear that it was a false alarm."

Mike patted his friend gently on the shoulder. "We did this because you're an essential part of the group, Phil. We also wanted to show you that we can and will act decisively."

Then he gave Phil a firm look with his single blue eye and his tone was harsher. "There's something else you and Sheila both need to understand, so listen up! Neither of you has ever asked why I never married. You two persuaded me to sacrifice something for the cause. I should never have agreed. My guilt and regrets prey on me all the time. They'll never go away. I betrayed the love of my life, Sarah Cohen. She was a true revolutionary, not some toffee nosed dilettante like half of our comrades, or a Champagne socialist like Sheila."

"Sarah told me what the Nazis did to her people. In her memory, I will ruthlessly eliminate any such resurgence, wherever and whenever it starts. I did this for her as well as for you!" Mike got up and stalked out, leaving the door open.

Phil sat for half an hour, head down and crying, with his shoulders heaving. Then he stared at the empty table for a while. He struggled with the turmoil of his conflicting emotions. He was furious that his chance of personal revenge and redemption had been snatched from his grasp. He felt new guilt about how he and Sheila pushed Mike into betraying Sarah. Mike was a true friend. Finally, Phil cried for his aunt and father.

Wrung out of all emotion by his grief, finally he stood up and dried his eyes on a tissue. He hardened his heart for what was to come. Then he strode purposefully out to find his ride. There was still a revolution to arrange.

CHAPTER 9
RICH MAN POOR MAN

"The form of association, however, which must be expected to predominate, is not that which can exist between a capitalist as chief, and workpeople without a voice in the management, but the association of the laborers themselves on terms of equality, collectively owning the capital with which they carry on their operations, and working under managers elected and removable by themselves."

John Stuart Mill

A hotel meeting room in London, May 2014

In the meeting room of a central London hotel, the documentary producer sat alongside his lead reporter. He glared at Lord Stoodley across the table. Mike was wearing his black eye patch.

"Look, Lord Stoodley. I do want to make a documentary about your company. And you damned well know why. Viewers have the right to know what foreign wars, assassinations and the like are being funded by our own and foreign governments through your business.

Mike smiled benignly back at him. He held his hands, palms up in a conciliatory gesture. "Please call me Mike; everyone does. Now I invited *you* here, because I want a documentary made about my company. You in particular mind, not some right wing apologist for the establishment. Have you asked yourself why?'

Only a little disarmed, the producer said, "Well, why don't you tell us, er, Mike."

"It's because I have some things I want investigated by someone with a critical eye. There are ideas we need to get out into the public domain for the future good of the whole country."

"It sounds like you want some kind of PR crap for a public share offering or something. Well, we're not about to whitewash a bunch of contract killers, just so you can make even more money!"

Mike looked him steadily in the eye. "Good! That's exactly the attitude I hoped for. Now let me explain."

The producer was on a roll and infuriated by Mike. He was nothing like he expected. He burst in, "Come on I want to do a full expose on your business, no holds barred."

The lead reporter put a restraining hand on his boss's arm and said, "Let's hear what Mike has to say."

* * *

That September, Sheila, Phil and Mike sat in the home entertainment room of Lambeth Palace, the London residence of the Archbishop of Canterbury. A handsome deacon walked over, giving Phil a meaningful look, and refreshed Sheila's glass of brandy. Phil watched him appreciatively as he left the room.

Phil clicked on the big screen with the remote control. While the dramatic signature music of the investigative program played, the screen filled with a mix of soldiers; explosions, obviously foreign faces of women and children cringing in horror; bodies lying by the roadside; wailing Islamic women and then Mike's smiling face with his signature eye patch.

Sheila groaned, "Jesus, Mike this is terrible! What have you done?"

"Watch!" said Mike.

The reporter appeared on the screen to set the scene. Images of computers, tough looking and very alert men in suits, helicopters, shooting ranges and armored vehicles charging through mud, appeared as background.

"This report is about a four billion pound business. The holding company has no easily identifiable name. I'm talking about a business with elements operating in many international war zones. It advises governments and mega corporations on physical and cyber security. It freely admits that it employs computer hackers and electronics warfare specialists. It has access to the darkest secrets of governments and security agencies. It provides contract personnel as bodyguards and military advisors on the ground. Some would call them mercenaries."

"Its personnel are often armed. Many of its employees are recruited from the British, US and other special forces. It is by far the most secretive organization we've ever investigated."

The camera focused back on Mike. "Many of you will recognize Lord Stoodley. He received a Military

Cross for bravery in our Falklands War against Argentina. At that time, he was a captain in the SAS, the Special Air Service.

The camera briefly showed the winged dagger badge of the SAS with its motto ' *Who dares Wins.*'

"He prefers to be called Mike. We are here in his modest farmhouse, somewhere in the Yorkshire Dales. The camera showed some views across open countryside, with drystone walls dividing the fields. Sheep were grazing in the distance. "Mike, you are obviously a very wealthy man. Why do you live in such a rustic setting and in such a modest house?"

"Well, Brian, it's easy to ensure security when you are far from any neighbors. As to the size of the place, it is all I need. You'll find that as chief executive and original owner of the business I pay myself less than many of our employees. I don't need more and don't see why I should expect more."

"Mike, do you seriously expect the viewers to believe that you don't receive payments offshore or have other more luxurious houses hidden away through secret trusts?"

"Believe it or not, Brian, it happens to be true. Some of our businesses need safe houses and bases for some of our activities, but they are all functional and rather Spartan. Besides, I rarely visit them, as others lead our operations on the ground nowadays."

"Well, that takes me to another point. There've been rumors that your people are involved in kidnappings, assassinations and illegal attacks on foreign soil, without the knowledge of the governments in question. What do you say to that?"

Phil looked worried. "Hell, Mike, why did you do this?"

"Watch!" said Mike.

Back on the screen, he replied, "Obviously, for client security and the safety of our personnel, we could not allow you complete access to our field operations. We did let your team visit and film at some of our training facilities in the US and the UK. This was on condition that you didn't give away their locations or the identity any of our people."

"Despite your awards for being the best investigative reporting team in the world, you could not find a single instance of any law breaking by any of our people anywhere. You brought us two alleged cases. We were able to prove to you that they were conducted by other organizations. Neither of them has anything to do with us. One is a US organization and the other is based in the Crimea. Perhaps investigating them further might reveal what you are looking for."

Brian shot back, "Well, if it's not to make money for you, Mike, what exactly is your business for?"

"Good question, Brian. Firstly, our aim is to support firms and democratic countries in avoiding terrorist and criminal disruption. Secondly, we want to demonstrate that it is possible to operate a corporation, owned for its employees."

"You are claiming that your business is owned by its employees."

"Not claiming Brian, it is. We looked around at many types of organization. In particular we evaluated two types of co-operative. One type is owned by its commercial participants. Agricultural co-ops, run by farmers are like this."

"Why not use that approach then?"

"Because though many function reasonably effectively, we found none that compete on the international scale that we have, and with traditionally organized firms."

"OK, what is the other type of co-op?"

"It's an organization operated on behalf of its customers. The UK's co-operative movement has many examples. I once thought that giving back profits to customers in that way was a formula for success, but in every endeavor the UK co-op has been out-competed by traditional firms."

"And why is that?"

"Various reasons. A major one is that too many decisions have been made, based on traditional Labour Party dogma, rather than business grounds. The place is full of minor Labour Party functionaries with little knowledge of business. Decisions are slow. Top people are chosen because of their politics, not their ability. This resulted in a major scandal this year. The chairman of the Co-operative Bank was spending the Co-op's money on rent boys and his drug habit. He got the job on purely political grounds."

Sheila erupted. "You bastard, Mike! Labour is my party!"

Phil calmed her, gently patting her hand. "No, it isn't Sheila. The Labour Party is only a cover for our real plans. Let's watch the rest."

On screen, Mike continued. "We also looked at giving the shares to the employees. That doesn't outlast the first generation of employee owners. The first chance to cash in their shares they sell out to the highest bidder. That simply returns the firm back to capitalist ownership."

Brian interrupted. "So which type of organization did you choose?"

We've adopted an approach that has proved successful, both in Scandinavia and here in the UK. It's a similar structure to that of the tremendously successful and respected John Lewis Partnership. John Lewis runs department stores and Waitrose supermarkets throughout England. It competes effectively with traditionally owned large firms like Harrods, the House of Fraser, Tesco, Sainsbury, Walmart and the like."

"So how will that work for you?"

"Brian, we put our firm's shares in a perpetual trust. They are owned on behalf of all current employees. The shares cannot be sold and do not belong to individual employees. The profit from the business is divided into shares. Much is reinvested. A significant share is issued as bonuses to all employees. Each person gets the same percentage of his or her salary as bonus. There is no question of the top level of management claiming they did it all themselves. Some is donated to genuine charities. None goes to political parties."

"What about the interests of customers?"

"Our approach motivates everyone to make a profit. You cannot do that if you do not satisfy customers and be better than competitors. No profits, no bonuses! My people were even keen to save electricity by turning off lights, when no one is in a room. Now, of course, we use smart systems to do all that."

"Our management is carefully selected by the professionals in the business. Top positions, apart from mine, pay well but not as well as those in the competing companies, which we outperform. We don't want our people to be mainly motivated by money. We do bring in outstanding people in the middle of the business, but to rise to the top, they have to deliver."

"If this is such a great system, how come all businesses don't adopt it?"

"That's simple. It requires the original owners, in this case me, to donate the firm to the trust and not to interfere in the future generations of leadership. That will never happen with firms being run for their shareholders and managements. Sadly, too many business owners fail to see that their success is built on the efforts of others as well as themselves. Their success is largely due to luck. They were lucky to be born in the right country, with the right genes and to have had education and experience that one way or another makes them successful."

"How do the employees feel about this system?"

"Well, you have met many of them and they were able to share their views with you. We introduced an employee run internal paper, 'The Insider'. This is run free from management interference and publishes the views of employees, without censorship. For example, if managers are observed having over-lavish entertainment, that can be reported."

"So are you going to step down?"

"Yes, I will, but not quite yet. There are still some things I want to achieve. You will have to wait to see what they are."

The rest of the program tried to throw mud at several of Mike's companies, but with limited success.

* * *

Phil said, "So we should plan to operate a variation on typical capitalist competition, but with confiscation of big businesses and running them as trusts for the employees."

"Exactly, and there are real examples to show that it works, including my own business! My economists have built a model of the future UK economy. It comprises a thousand large businesses, operating as employee trusts. There'll be several thousand middle-sized businesses, owned by entrepreneurs and stockholders, in the usual way. A planned UK sovereign wealth fund will be an investor in many of them. Then there'll be many thousands of smaller businesses. In many ways, they will be the most dynamic part of the economy and drive growth and employment."

Sheila said, "Well, it sounds very plausible, let's hope we can make it work."

Mike said confidently, "The model of the economy and my gut business feelings both say that it will."

Chapter 10
Branding and Spin

"I can hear the philosophers protesting that it can only be misery to live in folly, illusion, deception and ignorance, but it isn't -it's human."

Erasmus

Phil called the next meeting at Gayhurst. Mike thought Phil seemed more focused than the last time he saw him. Getting Paraguay out of his head had certainly worked.

Phil smiled a little sheepishly as he began, "I hate to be the one to bring this forward, but Revolution has been cancelled."

Sheila and Mike looked at each other, puzzled, trying to see if the other one got the joke. Phil chuckled at their discomfort. "I struggled with my own thoughts, ideals and conscience before I brought this to the table. I've taken a leaf out of your world of business, Mike. Some associates of mine conducted a number of surveys using untraceable websites and tweets. We wanted to see what the brand 'Revolution' meant to the mass of the people in Britain. We wanted to discover what would bring the people of Britain onto the streets to support a new regime. Sad to say, but the result was a resounding raspberry for 'Revolution.'"

"Like all political words, Revolution is polysemic, depending who you talk to."

"What the hell does that mean?" asked Mike.

Sheila answered before Phil got a chance, "You absolute peasant, Mike! It means that different people see different meanings in the same word."

She puffed herself up and continued, while Mike and Phil concealed their smirks at her pomposity. "Political words are also memes. A meme is a single word that can convey a whole idea and shared culture of meaning. 'Mafia' is a good example."

"Thank you, Sheila" said Phil, handing round some papers. "You can see here what people associated with the word 'Revolution'. Eighty-five percent feel negatively about it. They see it as bringing 'violence' 'destruction' 'radical change' 'Communism.'"

"Probing more deeply, we found that most people, especially women, felt that 'Revolution' threatened their families, their homes and their savings. It brings major uncertainty and risk".

Sheila looked pensive, "Mmm. We shouldn't really be surprised. Many, or even most, revolutions have been exactly like that. Furthermore, there's been a hundred years of capitalist propaganda to drive those thoughts home."

Phil went on, "Hang on, there's more. If you look at page two, we asked about the associations of other political words. 'Nazism' and 'Communism' are both badly regarded by most, as you might expect. Even the word 'Socialism' is seen simply a synonym for 'Communism' to many. There is a significant minority who embrace socialism to varying degrees, but there is also a disturbingly large minority supporting fascist ideas, if not the word Nazi."

"The next paragraph should interest you, Sheila. The poor response to the brand 'Labour Party' and similarly 'New Labour' surprised us. There were many negative feelings. Most people see Labour as a party for blue-collar workers and trade unionists, in other words, for people unlike their self-images. The UK population sees itself as overwhelmingly middle class. 'Labour' has an image rooted in the long distant past, of the workhouse, child labour, great depressions, state intervention and general strikes. The majority of voters feel threatened by this party. They fear higher taxes, restrictions on their freedom and rule by extremist trade unionists and bureaucrats."

Mike remarked, "Well, that makes sense as well. What conclusions do you draw from this, Phil?"

"Let me cover the rest before we get to that, Mike. As you can imagine, my socialist principles were severely challenged by these findings. On the positive side, you can see on pages three and four that 'the Conservative Party' is equally badly regarded. It is seen as being run by and for the rich establishment, *a party for toffs and celebs* and *out of touch with the needs of most people.* The opinions on the major parties match those from most published opinion polls and show why so few bother to vote in elections. Most voters see no party as representing their needs."

"Pages five and six show how people feel about other political words. 'Liberal' is now seen by many as a synonym for 'left wing' or 'socialist'. Neither of these words encourages wide spread support. In the UK, the existence of the wishy-washy Liberal Democratic

Party weakens the word further. Despite this, 'democratic' has a generally positive image here in the UK, though we understand that in the US, many, especially Republicans, see it as meaning 'socialist.'

"Now to your question, Mike, I'm afraid we need to completely change the branding of our 'Revolution.' Indeed, that's the last thing we can call it. The best thing we can do is to spin our propaganda so as to appear to be against those wicked revolutionaries. We should paint unnamed others as being responsible for all the violence and mayhem that brings about the planned situation. We should appear as knights in shining armor, riding in to rescue society from anarchy and restoring order, economic prosperity, democracy and the prosperity of the middle class. If we do these things, the people of Britain will come out on the streets in our support."

"I love it!" exulted Sheila. 'We can be seen as the counter revolutionaries and emerge to rule, free from the stain and taint of the bloody revolution which we created!"

Mike chipped in, "This means that from this day onwards, we have to train ourselves to drop all references to 'revolution,' 'socialism' and all related words. We can no longer refer to anyone as 'Comrade,' 'Brother' or 'Sister.' We need to carefully plan everything we say and do."

Sheila snorted, slapping the table for emphasis. "So what's new? We just have to act like we politicians do already. Every sound bite and phrase has to be spun and carefully scripted."

Phil said, "There is one last unpalatable finding. See there on page seven, second paragraph, sixty percent of the people value the monarchy. Most realize that it is costly and adds no value to politics, but they simply like it. As we plan to wipe out all those in line to the throne, we need to be totally thorough in that."

Sheila sat up trying to look regal and patted her hair, "Well, maybe we can give them what they want. I would look quite well in a crown, don't you think?"

Phil glanced darkly at Mike, "Sometimes, Sheila, I think you should be one of those going up against the wall."

She fixed him with her famously steely stare, "Never forget, my faux Archbishop, that you need a legitimately elected politician with a credible track record to make all of this work. Maybe I'll send *you* to the wall one day."

Phil forced a smile, but his eyes were unsmiling.

* * *

After Sheila left, Phil hung back to speak with Mike. He felt closer to him since their discussions after the Paraguay revenge mission. "Sheila sounded as though she might seriously like to be a queen. What did you think?"

"Don't worry, Phil. Remember that there are three of us. We can curb her most grandiose ideas. Besides, she was right, we need an elected politician to be credible with the public."

"Well, I am worried. The politburo felt it could keep Stalin in check. So did the old guard industrialists and politicians, with Hitler, and look what happened to them."

"You're right, Phil, we do need to keep an eye on her."

"Another thing, Mike, We really need to finish our plans and act. You've no idea how impatient I'm getting."

"I understand that, Phil, and we all feel the same way. I promised to come with more detailed plans and they will be ready in just three more weeks. Trust me."

"I do, Mike, but I'm less sure about Sheila."

CHAPTER 11
FINAL PLANNING
AND PLOTTING

"Fools learn by experience. I prefer to learn from the experience of others."

Otto von Bismarck

True to his word, Mike called another clandestine meeting at Gayhurst House, but five rather than three weeks later. Phil and Mike arrived before Sheila. Phil said, "It's not like you to delay a meeting by two weeks. Why the postponement?"

"Wait till you see Sheila and you'll understand."

Sheila arrived wearing huge dark glasses and looking unusually fragile. Phil asked, "Are you ill, Sheila?"

"No. I just have a bad hangover," she retorted testily. When she visited the loo, Mike quietly explained. "You've pointed out before that none of us is getting any younger and I notice that you've been tinting your hair, Phil. Well, Sheila has been for a facelift coupled with a detox."

Phil smirked and said, "How on earth did you know that? She really does need to lay off the sauce, though."

"It's my job to keep a protective eye on you all, Phil."

Still wearing the sunglasses, Sheila re-entered the room, lit a cigar and poured herself a large glass of port, before taking her seat. Gesturing with the cigar, she asked Mike morosely, "All right, now that we're all settled, what have you got for us?"

Mike plugged a hard drive into his computer. The images filled the big plasma screen on the wall.

"We've made some video of our analysis. To liven it up, we've included clips from some interesting cases. As you know, every policy option is connected to every other policy. We had to begin somewhere. I've started with the distribution of wealth and inheritance. It seems to be the key to the whole economic puzzle."

Phil grunted. "Well, as long as we include sorting out the greedy bankers and improving the lot of the masses, I guess that's as good a place to start as any."

The video started. One of Mike's young MBAs introduced herself as the narrator. She talked as the first chart filled the screen. *"This pie chart shows that from a UK population of sixty-five million, the poorest half of households only own ten percent of the wealth. Poorer households are larger. We estimate that on a per capita basis the top ten percent of the population owns more than fifty percent of the wealth in the UK.*

"Our research shows that globally just over one hundred people own more than the poorest third of the world population. We have a global list of five thousand rich people. Over half of them are multi- billionaires. They effectively control the world.

"Wealth is insidious. It creates privilege down the generations. It bypasses attempts to curb it with inheritance laws. That's why the names Rockefeller, Ford, Rothschild, Grosvenor, Windsor and many others keep popping up over many generations. These people held the keys to power and wealth through past generations, and will for those to come."

"Hang on!" Phil interjected. "I know of the Fords, Hiltons and Rockefellers. Windsor presumably refers to the British Royals, but who the hell are the Grosvenors?"

Mike paused the video.

Sheila said, "Come on, Phil, you must have heard of the Dukes of Westminster. They were lucky enough to own half of the west end of London when it was just farming land in the 17th Century. Now that that it's the world's prime real estate, they still do."

They returned their eyes to the screen. Mike restarted the video and the MBA narrator continued, "To bring this alive, we taped a number of interviews. First up is Lady Jessop, wife of City banker Sir Ronald Jessop."

The movie showed a large, sandstone mansion built in acres of exquisitely manicured gardens and rolling parkland. A silver Rolls Royce Phantom stood next to a metallic blue Aston Martin Virage on the spacious forecourt, at the end of the stately drive. Cutting to a spacious room furnished with superb antiques, they saw an elegantly dressed and immaculately coiffured Lady Jessop. A large Rembrandt in a heavy gilded frame was visible behind her. She smiled graciously. "Well, dear, I'm delighted to be able to appear in one of Mike's videos. Here are my thoughts on the questions you sent me."

"Both our families worked hard over several generations to earn what we have. Yes, it's true that we both had wealthy parents, but my husband, Ronnie, worked hard at Eton. He was clever enough to get into Oxford. Then he did rather well in the bank. He was chosen as chairman, purely on merit. He followed on from my father, you know."

"We feel that we give a lot to the UK. The bank employs over 60,000 staff. Our personal estates and properties here and overseas employ nearly a thousand more. We keep the UK economy working by funding mortgages, businesses and international trade. We are a huge positive for the balance of payments."

"As you know, our children are really intelligent. They are doing brilliantly at good prep schools. They will go on to Eton and be well fitted to inherit all of this when the time comes." She waved to her elegant surroundings. We see it as our duty to keep up these great old houses. No one else would."

"You asked what would happen if there were a wealth tax? That would be so unfair you know. After all, people like Ronnie have to be rewarded for the financial risks they take. He says that the top few percent of people like us pay most of the taxes in the UK. We give so much and get back so little. Anyway, we could easily move offshore. Ronnie could work in New York or Hong Kong. Then what would the UK do? Besides, most of our money is in offshore trusts for the children. We can't touch it. Neither can the taxman."

Mike smiled, as he saw both Sheila and Phil bridling and restraining themselves from major outbursts.

Phil grumbled, "Same in Paraguay, same everywhere."

As the video moved on to an interview with a business leader receiving 300 times more than his least paid employee, Phil was beside himself. "We should just round the bastards up and shoot 'em!"

After a number of similar interviews, Doreen appeared on the screen. She was a single mother living on welfare in one room. She was obese, heavily tattooed, smoking a joint and breastfeeding the most recent of her five children. The others were squabbling loudly all around her. "What chance did we ever have? Mi dad beat mi ma. He left when she caught him interferin' with me. We get what we can from the social, but it's all crap. Yes, I smoke and drink and do a little blow. How else am I supposed to get through the fuckin' days?"

There were other interviews. Some showed patently fit people receiving disability benefits. Others portrayed young couples struggling to save a deposit for a house. Some interviewees didn't want to work, but had figured how to play the system so they did not need to.

Mike appeared on the screen, "The bottom line is that if we take from the wealthy and use the money to fund education and better welfare for the poor, things will change. We have to ensure that those who can work do work. No one rips off the system. Here's our proposal.

"We already have records of who owns what and where. Much of it is hidden offshore and in trusts. My cyber warfare hackers are really good at this sort of thing. If we want to, we can simply transfer funds from the hidden and supposedly secret accounts. We've been helping the British Government to intercept and filch Al-Qaeda and ISIS funds for years. We can do it that way, but there is a more effective way, to ensure we have everything".

"We round up the billionaires, the bankers and land owners. We sit 'em down one by one and make the following offer. *'You and your family are forbidden to leave the country for the time being. You will pass over 90% of everything you have right now. If you try to hide it or move any of it, we'll know. In that case you will then be sent to trial in a people's court. You and your family might be confined for re-education. You will be pilloried in the media as greedy, undeserving lawbreakers. All that you have will be confiscated. In egregious cases the courts may decide that you must suffer severer penalties."*

"Some of these people may be abroad. We'll hunt 'em down and bring 'em back. The Americans taught us all about 'extraordinary rendition', also known as 'kidnapping'.

"Once everyone gets used to the idea that great wealth is unacceptable, we can become more like Scandinavia. Those economies work pretty well."

"Inheritance greater than the average family possesses will be forbidden. There'll be no evasion through trusts or any other fancy schemes. All hidden funds and assets will be forfeit. On the same theme, no member of a family may be employed in a family-owned or controlled firm with sales greater than five million."

Sheila and Phil both looked pleased. Mike paused the video, "You'll like the next part, Phil; it harks back to part of what you presented five weeks ago."

He restarted the video and the MBA narrator reappeared and continued, "No one could argue that the people in this video are stereotypical. They are typical. We recorded hundreds of similar interviews and these are statistically representative of the whole sample."

"Here are some more charts, showing an analysis of the UK media from last March. The most read or seen items refer to The Royal family, society people and celebs. They dominate the front pages."

Various newspaper headlines appeared on the screen. Well-dressed celebs and royals posed smugly in designer cloths and exotic surroundings. Wimbledon, the King's box at the Derby, and yachts in Monaco were all featured. Other news items appeared lower down the illustrative front pages.

> **'Fifty thousand killed in Indian quake'**
> **'Bus Crash, 40 children dead'**
> **'US Drone blows up 50 civilians at Yemeni wedding'**
> **'North Korea tests Hydrogen bomb'**

"The British see the Royals and other celebs as providing a soap opera. They want to keep these soaps. It's illogical when you look at the facts, but it's just part of our culture."

Mike paused the video again when he saw Sheila wincing. He surmised she really did want to displace the Royals with herself. "You might not like it, Sheila, but the majority of folk live their lives by vicariously enjoying the success, wealth and yes, the downfall of these parasites. For their parts the Royals and celebs believe they earn or simply deserve all the wealth and adulation that falls to them. Sadly, this underpins the lifestyle and sense of entitlement that we saw earlier."

When he restarted the video Mike continued, appearing now on the big screen. "Well, our revolution, or as we will refer to its results, after Phil's banning of that word, our 'changes', will already have eliminated all near relatives of the Royal Family. Any left will be in hiding. There'll always be some obscure royal popping up and claiming the right to the UK throne. Of course they can be dealt with on a case by case basis."

"To deal with lords and ladies and all that snobbery, we were inspired by the 19th Century Gilbert and Sullivan Operetta, 'The Gondoliers'. In that Victorian comedy, the egalitarian gondoliers make everyone kings, queens and what have you. Based on that idea, here are our concrete proposals on honors and titles. Firstly, any citizen can choose any title he or she prefers to be addressed by. This will quickly eliminate, by opening to ridicule, all noble titles."

Sheila interrupted him, laughing and jabbing her cigar towards him, "No more Lord Stoodley then?"

"That's right, Sheila, I might prefer Duke of Stoodley, but the Archbish. here is safe. We'll keep functional titles, but the silly practice of having bishops in the legislature by right will go"

"Excellent!" exclaimed Phil.

Mike continued. "Secondly, we will create medals for those who genuinely contribute to public welfare. But there'll be no more silly Knighthoods, awarding of the Order of the British Empire and the like. The thirteenth century and suits of armor are ancient history and the Empire is long gone too."

"Thirdly, celebs, sports players and movie stars can have as much publicity as they and the people want. However if they crash their Ferraris whilst on cocaine or break the law in anyway, they will be given exemplary sentences. There will be no special treatment, such as they get now. The public likes to build 'em up, but also to see 'em fall."

The narrator continued, "We've concluded that the biggest problem in our society is the motivation of its leadership. Here's an interview with Professor of Psychology Bruce Mackenzie."

The learned Scottish professor was interviewed in his study at his University in Durham. He was balding and grey bearded. Blue eyes sparkled with intelligence behind his wire-rimmed glasses. He wore a tweed jacket with leather patches on the elbows. He spoke with a Scottish burr. "You see the problem with leaders is that their motivation is all wrong. Politicians are convinced that they know best how to spend other peoples' money. Business leaders see any success as due to their efforts. Any failures are blamed on lesser beings, lower down the pecking order."

"Our research shows what common sense tells you. They're usually narcissistic, meaning they are desperate to be admired. This often plays out as a hunger for power and all that comes with it."

Phil looked at Sheila, who nodded sagely, obviously excluding herself from such comments.

The professor continued. "Many business leaders, as well as politicians, are simply sociopaths. They want to control everything and to decide everything. They feel nothing for the pain and suffering of others. They are skilled at manipulating everyone to get what they want."

Phil held up a hand for Mike to pause the video. "A question Mike, what's the difference between a sociopath and a psychopath?"

Mike answered, "Good question Phil. The prof says that most psychologists use the words interchangeably. Some try to differentiate between the two, by ascribing the cause to genetic or trauma for psychopaths and nurture or experiential issues for sociopaths and then trying to ascribe nuances of behavior to each type. For our purposes it doesn't matter. Both don't feel for others. They disregard laws and social codes in their own behavior; never feel remorse or guilt and often display violent tendencies."

Mike restarted the video and the professor appeared on the screen again "Fortunately there are well respected psychometric tests for these things. They are hard to fool and can identify both sociopathy and narcissism. Our proposal is to screen all holders of political, official and senior business office for these traits, before they can even be considered as candidates for higher leadership roles. Those who care for the good of society as a whole and have empathy with the suffering of the disadvantaged will become more successful."

"Just a minute," said Sheila "Don't some psychopaths serve a useful purpose? If we were in a war, or more topically a revolution, would it not be useful to have some utterly ruthless people available to get the dirty work done?"

"The professor discussed all that with me," said Mike. "He told me that there was some evidence that heart surgeons were usefully psychopathic. The idea is that the best of them of them have no feelings of empathy with the patients' pains or potential deaths. They will therefore carve away at their hearts, taking lifesaving risks, whereas otherwise the patients would simply die. He also said that some claim that stock traders and other financial market makers take huge risks and earn large returns, because they have no care for the potential losses of the widows' and orphans' funds that they manage."

Phil interjected with a snort, "That's exactly why so many of those banker bastards go bad!"

Mike held up his hand. "Steady on, Phil, the prof also warned me about being too Panglossian."

"You made that word up, Mike!" accused Sheila.

"Aha, caught you with a word you don't know at last," laughed Phil. "I assume we are talking of Dr. Pangloss from Moliere's *Candide*, Mike?"

Mike could not resist smiling at Sheila's obvious chagrin. "We are indeed and in this case the professor warned us to beware of the fallacy that many evolutionary psychologists fall into. Dr. Pangloss argued that all things have a reason, so he invented a few and they were largely absurd. For example, he claimed that we have legs mainly so we can wear trousers. Sociopaths might make great generals or surgeons, but it is as likely that their lies and deception help them to be more successful in reproduction as much as for any other reason for the survival of the sociopathic gene. Besides some women seem to like bad men and men very often like wicked women."

Sheila cheered up. "There's still hope for me then."

Mike continued to lead discussion of his proposals for the whole weekend. The others revised a few points, but they ended with a general consensus and program.

Phil had added some of his ideas. "Over the years I've finally accepted that advertising and public relations are necessary, but only as long as they just inform the public of advantages and facts. I want us to include laws that ensure that corporations, the media and the advertising companies are forbidden from falsifying and twisting facts. The penalties need to be simple, draconian and easily enforced.

"Also the power of the industrial military complex to control the world through lobbying has to cease. Any official caught in corruption, as well as the person offering an inducement, will both be severely punished. It will never be acceptable for officials from government to take jobs in firms that have supplied them or any other branch of government, nor to act as self-employed advisors. To end this subtle form of corruption, we need to break the cozy interchange of public servants with industry."

* * *

Mike suggested that they take a break, so he led them on a walk in the sunshine from Gayhurst House and into the surrounding parkland, crossing the cattle grid. A group of red poll cattle were ruminating lazily in the heat of the day.

Leading the way, Mike took a footpath alongside the second of the Gayhurst lakes. A fisherman was busily landing a large carp from his spot on the far side of the lake and did not notice them. They struck out across a field and connected to a gravel farm track.

Sheila moaned. "Hey, Mike, I thought we were going for a stroll not a route march!"

"It's not too far and I want to show you something," said Mike.

The farm track turned sharply and passed through a sturdy concrete tunnel under the M1 motorway, with its noisy traffic. Then it skirted wheat fields, passing a farmhouse with its grain silos and entered a wood-land nature reserve. Mike led them through the trees and then onto a footpath through more fields, where sheep were grazing. Sheila looked hot and bothered at the unaccustomed exercise. "Just a short way to go," said Mike cheerily.

Phil looked round and noticed a mini-drone following their progress. He turned angrily on Mike. "Jesus, Mike, I am sick to my back teeth with you watching everything we do! People need their privacy! What kind of nasty Big Brother regime are we going to emplace?"

Mike smiled at him, "You're quite right, Phil. Believe me, we need to use these drones and all kinds of intercepts now and until the new regime is stable. Then we'll cut it back."

Phil looked skeptically at him and spoke gruffly, "Well, you'd better. That stuff drives most people crazy."

They walked on and as they came to the edge of a spinney, they could see a huge compound across more fields. It had a high linked fence topped with razor wire. Security cameras, mounted at intervals, scanned all round the modern and extensive buildings inside. Large arrays of radio masts, hundreds of feet tall, were moored with wires to stabilize them against the wind. "We won't go further in case we appear on their CCTV," said Mike. "What do you think of that place?"

"It's huge. What on earth is it?" asked Phil. "I didn't see it marked on the map of the area."

Mike replied, "It's a Government Communications listening and analysis complex. It scoops electronic communications of all kinds from the air. It's linked to others in the UK, the US and bases all around the world. There is a big one in Cyprus, for example. Any phone call, text, e-mail, tweet or social media entry can be collected, analyzed and stored. Gayhurst happens to be right next to it, but there is no escape from the reach of Britain's Government Communications Headquarters, 'GCHQ' and its sister in the US, the NSA."

"Bloody hell!" said Phil, "It must cost millions. How can they cope with the sheer volume of data?"

Mike laughed, "More like billions, but most of the funding is secret. They have linked super computers scanning all messages for key words and others focused on specific targets. The whole thing is so secret no one knows what privacy and other laws it violates. Nothing and no one anywhere in the world can escape the scrutiny of this little beauty and its sisters. That is why we never communicate electronically with each other and are super careful about arranging our little gatherings, cloaking everything we do in innocent words and activities. Of course, I employ a team of 'sweepers' to clean any data about us that might cause suspicion. "

From the cover of the trees, Sheila swept Mike's binoculars over the facility, saying, "Wow! I want one!"

"And you shall have this one!" said Mike, smiling. "And all the rest. Some of my people have been placed on the inside. My firm has government contracts to help develop the technology. We get the highest security clearance. Others among our employees are regularly hacking into any systems we don't have access to. These include the equivalent agencies in Russia, China and Israel. When the time comes, this is a key target for us to temporarily disable and then to control for our own purposes."

Phil retorted, "But it all has to be drastically cut back when we've won."

As they walked back to Gayhurst, Mike proudly described some of his other activities. "We have broken into many sites in the 'Darknet'. Some of the media call it by various other names, but it is little understood. Think of the Internet as a deep ocean. Search engines like Google and Yahoo are like fishing boats trawling for data. Their web crawlers act like trawl nets, scanning for key words. In the depths, beneath their reach are encrypted messages and hidden networks programed to be inaccessible in order to avoid detection. Think of them as rather like super stealthy submarines. Initially, the CIA and the military set some up to protect their most secret communications. Very quickly the money launderers, gangsters and drug cartels saw the potential opportunity. They use encrypted programs to avoid detection and Bitcoins and other Internet currencies to bypass banking regulations. We've developed means to detect hidden Internet traffic and then we hack into those hosting and using the Darknet. We really can see almost everything."

* * *

On returning from their walk and after a box lunch, the trio reached firm consensus on policies to be implemented after they had seized power. Then Phil chimed in with his show stopping question, "OK, we will have great policies when we have seized power. The big outstanding issue is how do we justify the violence needed to seize and retain power? I'm not against necessary violence, but do any of us really want to go down in history as a Stalin, a Mao or a Hitler?"

They looked at each other uneasily. Sheila eventually broke the silence. "Well, we have dealt with that by our planned propaganda to blame others for the revolution and to position ourselves as the firm leadership that can restore order. But this is an important subject. We've all done some rough things, just to be where we are now. Let's get it on the table and thrash it out further. I propose that we take an hour's break to get our thoughts in coherent order."

* * *

Mike lay in his room on his bed. He typed his notes into an iPad.

Sheila went to the sitting room and thought, *'No need to think too hard about this one. Being the next Stalin might be fun. The boys can deal with masking it. When they done, I'll get rid of them.'*

She looked closely into the large, gilded baroque mirror. She saw a few bruises from her recent surgery and a few remaining wrinkles, making a mental note to schedule some more Botox treatment. Then walking over to the antique drinks cabinet, she poured herself a glass of deep red Petrus from a lead-crystal decanter, enjoying the thought that Mike and Phil would be furious if they knew the cost of it. She clipped the end of a Havana and lit it with a gold lighter.

Kicking off her shoes, she stretched her legs, crossing them at the ankle, lay back in her chair and blew a smoke ring. Through half closed eyes, she watched and admired it as it slowly expanded and floated towards the ceiling.

Phil scribbled busily on a writing pad in the meeting room. Occasionally he heavily underlined a point or scored something out.

* * *

After an hour, Sheila bellowed down the corridor in her best teacher's voice, "Come on, boys, time's up. Put your pens down."

They reassembled in the meeting room. "All right, who wants to be first?" demanded Sheila.

Mike made an exaggerated mock gesture towards Phil. "As this is mainly a moral question, we should give the floor to our reverend Bishop to go first."

Phil gave a little bow to Mike and presented his views. "There are two groups of people whose needs we must consider in this question. The first is the current Establishment. Directly or indirectly, in current or long past generations, many of its members have used the power of armed force to gain what they have.

All of them rely on their laws and their courts to protect their wealth. Failing that, they rely on the police and ultimately the army and security forces to keep any dangerous dissent at bay."

"Over and above these things, the forces of the state have bloodily suppressed the rights of those in many other countries in their attempts to win independence and rights to freedom through the centuries. We can say that the colonial era is long gone, but the damage done by Britain in China, India, Africa and many other places lives on. In modern times, British drones or troops were or are still used overtly to kill in Northern Ireland, Iraq and Afghanistan. They did the same covertly in many other places. Together with the US, the UK government sees itself as the world's policeman.

"Britain supports many bad regimes and special interests, as well as our ever aggressive US allies. British drones are rocketing innocents as 'collateral damage'. This happens every week and in all sorts of places that we have no right or business to be. These are war crimes. They have to stop and those responsible brought to justice."

"Our clandestine services and bases are involved in torture, extraordinary rendition and other unknown criminal acts. Mike knows about all this. I hope he feels suitably guilty! And yes, Mike, we know the documentary people didn't find anything. That's because you cover your tracks too well."

Mike gave Phil an affable wave of the hand, "OK, Phil, good points made. What is the second group of people we should be concerned with?"

"The oppressed masses, of course. They want to live in a decent and caring society. They don't want to feel they are run by a cruel and equally oppressive dictatorship. The vicious and bloody teeth of the current regime are well hidden behind a mask of gentile and quaint civilization."

"For this reason, we need to do the following. We must, quickly and ruthlessly and with all the violence necessary, create a new regime. We must use propaganda to avoid any association of the new regime with the violence that led to its inauguration. Then we must institute a post-revolutionary softer touch, as soon as possible."

Sheila could hold back no longer. Mike wondered how she had let others speak for so long. "OK, we lie to the people, just like all governments do and always have! In principal, I'm not against that. The trouble is that deceit is nearly always discovered. Also, don't think this will be over in a day. We've studied and

talked through enough revolutions to realize that survivors of those overthrown by revolution, or wanting
things run differently, come back with a counter-rev-
olution. They have to be dealt with, too. Still more violence! What do you think, Mike? You've supported
a few military coups in your time."

Mike deferred his answer, but took Sheila's invitation
to speak. "Phil's named two important groups and
you raise excellent questions, Sheila. There's another
group, critical to success. It includes all the forces
needed to support any regime: the military, the police and the civil service. Without control over these
we'll fail. It will be vital to give them the right motivation and leadership from the start."

"We'll also need to head off any interventions from
other countries. Our new regime not only needs to
change things here in the UK, but it also needs to kick
start the process elsewhere. We've already agreed
that land only belongs to populations by right of force
or inheritance, but nationality and territoriality are
deeply embedded by human evolution. We should
sow the seeds of change in other countries. If nothing
else, that will keep them from interfering in Britain."

"Phil's right too. Especially at the outset, we can't let
everyone know what's happening, who's responsible
and why. If we did, there'd be a backlash. Besides,

why telegraph our punches to the counter-revolutionaries?"

Phil interrupted. "There's one other question. We've only touched on it before. Why do we need to cause explosions that can kill innocent bystanders?"

Mike stepped in very firmly, with emphatic hand gestures to illustrate his points. "Our answer to that is twofold. We need explosions that go beyond the immediate area of the Royal convoy during the assassination. In the same way, the blasts need to extend beyond the immediate location of the funerals. The reason in both cases is that the explosions might be less successful than intended. Things rarely go completely according to plan."

"Chaos and destruction in a wider area will catch any early leavers or late arrivals, as well as hampering any rescue efforts. Pragmatically, we need the widespread fear that this will cause so that the public will accept the restrictions on their freedom that we will need to impose in the short term. Fear of terrorism and jihad has been used to cow the peoples of Europe and the US to accept incredible restrictions and intrusions into their privacy for years. We need to learn from the way the existing elites have manipulated this fear. "

Phil said, "My concern is still for the innocent civilians, especially at the funeral. There'll be a hell of a lot of 'em. How do you justify that? It'll hardly endear us to the ordinary people that we want on our side and for whom we're doing all this."

Sheila answered before Mike could make his second point. "Mike and I have discussed this. We need to shock the world, to add to the chaos. The people in the crowds will be die-hard royalists. Nothing will change that, except by letting them die, hard. We will simply oblige them." She chortled with glee. "It'll create mass aversion therapy to being anywhere near to any surviving Royals."

Phil looked at her askance. "There's a bit of the Nero in you, Sheila."

The discussion lasted late into the night. The weekend finished with broad agreement on all issues. Now all they had to do was to seize power.

CHAPTER 12
SEIZING CONTROL

'The world has come to such a state that one can no longer find anyone who does good.'

Savonarola, a reforming Florentine priest,
burnt at the stake in 1498

Struggling to recover from the effects of the massive explosions in and around Westminster Abbey, SAS Colonel Johnny Hammond shook his head to clear it. He clamped his jaw tight to help him overcome the pain in his arm by sheer will power. He pondered what to do. It was tempting to await first aid and let someone else worry. He dismissed that thought. Where would he and any troops he could gather, be needed most?

Deciding on a course of action, he staggered down a shattered staircase from his aerie in the Houses of Parliament. As he went, he collected his remaining men. They too were in shock. Some were wounded. The nearest exit at ground level was blocked by fallen masonry, but they found a way into the nearest street, Milbank, by following a rubble-strewn corridor and kicking a door outwards through its twisted frame.

Near the ruins of the Abbey, a Coldstream Guards major in his torn and dirty red dress uniform sat on a lower step. His bearskin headgear lay lower down, dusty and damaged. The red plume was just discernible. It was a miracle that he was alive and apparently uninjured. Hammond bawled at him. "Heads up, Major! You're coming with me."

"But, Sir, I need to find some of my men and await orders."

Hammond pointed his Heckler and Koch at the Guards officer meaningfully. The major got the message. He joined Hammond's growing and disparate band.

This rabble of battered warriors co-opted any others in uniform who could walk, as they stumbled over broken, fallen wreckage towards Parliament Square. The famed clock tower, Big Ben, was just a heap of fallen stones and twisted iron. Everywhere there were screaming people, choking with dust. Many were bleeding from horrific injuries. The dead lay all around, some bodies were in several pieces.

A young military policewoman, wearing a white-powdered red cap, broke ranks, trying to help a shrieking woman with blood pumping from the stump of her leg. Hammond barked, "Leave her! She's a goner. We have to ignore all this and keep our team together."

The policewoman went into shock and started wailing. Hammond's sergeant slapped her face. He bawled, "Pull yerself together, soldier, and do as you're fuckin' told!"

Then he chambered a round into his Browning automatic. He put the gun to the injured civilian's head and fired. She stopped shrieking and lay still. The shooter pushed the MP into line to follow the others. "It's best. She's out of her suffering now, girl."

Hammond halted at the far side of Parliament Square and addressed the fifty of so people he had assembled so far. With the leadership skills of a highly trained officer in a completely unknown and apparently hopeless situation, he confidently began. He had to shout loudly, as many were temporarily deafened. "Right! Here's the situation. You've all seen what happened. We have to expect chaos. We need to build strength and be prepared to defend against any further attacks."

"We're going to leave dealing with the injured to the fire brigade and ambulance people when they arrive. There's nothing we can do here." He looked meaningfully at the military police woman. Her lower lip was quivering. The gray ash on her cheeks was streaked by tears, but she held herself at attention.

"We need to get to 10 Downing Street. That's where the Prime Minister lives and that is where decisions will be made. Whoever is in charge will need our support."

"You men on the right will go with Sergeant Reed and round up more recruits. Those who are unarmed, pick up any weapons you can grab. Commandeer any armored vehicles. You, Corporal with that radio, keep trying to see if the military and police networks come back on."

"The rest of you follow me! We will all rendezvous in Downing Street at 14:30 hours."

At the entrance to Parliament Street, they found an abandoned Scimitar light reconnaissance tank and commandeered it. A stray member of the Household Cavalry became Hammond's driver. His horse had been blown from under him, but he was un-harmed. He had dumped his ceremonial burnished breastplate and his formerly shiny, now battered helmet with its horsehair plume. He was familiar with this vehicle, which the ceremonial household troops used in their combat roles. Hammond rode high in the open turret, so he could see clearly.

A movement from above caught his attention in the corner of his eye. He jerked his head around and saw a tiny four rotor mini drone, positioning itself to film his column's progress. He regarded it carefully, noting the camera lens embedded in a sort of swivel ball beneath its middle and the drab olive green color. Raising his automatic pistol and bracing it with his other hand, he sighted carefully and fired two rounds into it. It disintegrated into a cloud of plastic and electronic parts as the 9mm slugs tore its flimsy body to pieces. He thought, *'Who the hell was controlling that?'*

Hammond's convoy grew, with the addition of a couple of military three-ton trucks and some troops. They had been on standby in a quiet street away from the blast. Their junior officers were pleased to find a decisive leader.

A roadblock of two BMW police cars, manned by an officious police sergeant, barred their path just after

King Charles Street. He shouted to Hammond, "My orders are to stop anyone leaving this area until we know who's behind this."

After a brief yelling match, Hammond bellowed, "There's no time for this. Stand away from your vehicle."

The cops dived for cover, as a three round burst from the 30 millimeter automatic cannon, mounted in Hammond's turret, demolished one of the BMWs. It flew apart and off the road. Its petrol tank exploded in a ball of flame. A door panel fluttered downwards like an enormous butterfly. This had a salutary effect on the crowd and cops, who made themselves scarce. Engine roaring, the tank lurched forward, belching black exhaust fumes. Then, it smashed aside the other police car. The convoy forged onwards behind it. Swiveling his head, Hammond could see pillars of black smoke at all points of the compass.

For no apparent reason, the military and police communications came back on. Hammond's radio operator handed him the headset.

The networks were all reporting chaos. Apart from the complete shambles around the Abbey and Parliament, it seemed that there was extensive rioting and looting starting in Newham, Hackney, Brixton and other poorer areas of London.

Hammond's radio operator scanned the frequencies. Disjointed messages jammed the network. In the cities of Birmingham, Manchester, Liverpool and Glasgow people had taken to the streets. Mostly, they were shocked and seeking the reassurance of crowds, but many saw the chance to do as they liked. Shops selling alcohol and pubs were targeted first. There were widespread fires and inadequate resources to fight them. Hospitals were overloaded.

As they drove towards Downing Street, the tank pushed aside abandoned cars in its path. Grim faced, they forced their vehicles through the milling crowds. Many people were hysterical. Others were more belligerent, shouting for information. One of Hammond's SAS troopers jumped down from the tank. He smashed the butt of his MP5 sub machine gun into an especially obstreperous man's mouth. There was a crunch of broken teeth and jaw. As he went down, blood poured from his face. Others leapt back to let them pass. The tank jerked forward, crushing the fallen man's legs under its track.

Hammond's tank arrived at Downing Street. The anti-vehicle barriers were up, the tall gates shut. A nervous police inspector waving a pistol looked nervously at Hammond's looming tank and his fierce looking force, as it debouched from their assortment of vehicles. Hammond strode up to him and his worried looking policemen. "Right, I'm SAS Colonel Johnny Hammond. Who's in charge here?"

"I guess I am sir. What shall we do?"

"OK, I'm taking over here. Sergeant Gregg will secure the perimeter. Let's check out the command post in Number Ten and see what we can find out."

* * *

North of London, near Hertford, a matte black helicopter with no identification markings, a sleek EC155, circled once over Sheila Reynolds' halted road convoy. It settled behind a tumbledown drystone wall in an adjacent field. Its turbines were still running.

Sheila Reynolds's protection officer, Detective Sergeant Daniels, noticed that the Home Secretary did not look at all surprised by its arrival. She merely said, "Come on, Sergeant! It looks like help has arrived."

She set off walking to the open gate at the edge of the field. Five men wearing all black combat uniforms and balaclavas leapt from the chopper. Daniels and his three constables approached the aircraft ahead of her, pistols drawn, but pointing to the ground. The black clad soldiers shot each man in the forehead, before they could react. They crumpled to the ground.

Sheila coolly stepped over Sergeant Daniel's body, stepping on his dead hand, without looking down and clambered aboard the chopper. It immediately clattered upwards, tilting forward as it headed south, at low level and fast, skimming the tree tops and roofs of buildings.

* * *

In the bunker under 10 Downing Street, Johnny Hammond finally made contact with GCHQ, Britain's equivalent of the US's NSA. Its CO, General Roberts, was put through and took Hammond's situation report. They knew each other. "OK, Johnny, good show! You'd better sit tight till we know what's happening. Hold Downing Street and don't allow anyone to enter who's not a known member of the Cabinet."

"I reckon they're all dead, Sir."

"Well, we'll have to see. Meantime, all hell is breaking loose. We have our nuclear forces on full launch alert. Our intercepts say that the US, France, Russia, China, Israel and others are all doing the same. Let's hope no one lets them off the leash. Keep this channel open. I have to go. I'm trying to find out where our chain of command starts. All the heads of the General Staff were in the Abbey."

Next, Hammond finally reached his friend, Jack Brewer, head of Scotland Yard's Special Branch. Jack said, "Glad you're OK, Johnny. Remember our nets are not secure."

"Don't I fucking know it, Jack! What can you tell me?"

"Not much. We're still looking for leads. I'll come over there to see you. It's the only secure way to talk."

* * *

Jack Brewer's black Range Rover and Sheila Reynolds's helicopter both arrived near Downing Street at about the same time. Both parties and their escorts headed towards the gates blocking access. Recognizing the Home Secretary, Jack said, "Thank God you're safe, Ma'am. What happened?"

"I was stuck near Hertford. We were ambushed. People were killed. Let's talk inside."

Her escort left her at the gate and moved smartly off. Her chopper flew away, before Sergeant Gregg could move to draft its crew into his growing force. "Bugger! A chopper would have been useful!"

Sheila and Jack were ushered into the Number 10 bunker. Sheila Reynolds brusquely proceeded to take charge, as if such events occurred every day.

Four hours later, she had most of the UK's armed forces under her control. She had arranged for Lord Stoodley to be brought there, remarking, "Given that our protection and anti-terrorist forces have bollocksed everything up, let's see what Mike's people can do to help."

Johnny Hammond stiffened at the insult, but reflected that it was justified. Besides, he had worked with and liked Mike Stoodley. Mike's SAS background, the ex-Special Forces teams in his firm and his global information network could be invaluable assets.

Sheila rattled off orders. "I want to know where every single surviving military officer is, at and above the equivalent rank of brigadier. Find out where any government ministers and members of both houses of Parliament are. When they're located, order them to stay put. Use force if necessary. We can't have loose cannons wandering about and causing confusion. You know what members of Parliament are like. They just love to feel important and interfere. Useless fucking busybodies!"

This elicited some wry faces and sideways glances among those present.

"Also, find me the Archbishop of Canterbury. Has his plane landed? I understand he wasn't in the Abbey."

She barked out further instructions, "I want the Foreign Office to find out who is taking control in overseas governments, that have lost their leaders. Get me secure lines to all of them. Start with the US, then Russia, then China. I also want continuous updates on their domestic political situations. Is that clear?"

"Yes Ma'am".

Johnny Hammond looked at Jack Brewer. They both saw that there was a strong leader in charge. God knew what catastrophes Britain and the world might face next. Maybe she could hold things together.

* * *

Alone together later, Hammond asked Jack, "Still no ideas who's behind all this?"

Jack gave him a hard look, "No, but it might be good to find out who delivered the Home Secretary here. They don't seem to be around."

Hammond looked surprised. "Bloody Hell!"

CHAPTER 13
MANAGING THE
COUNTER REVOLUTION

"The attribute of popular government in revolution is at one and the same time virtue and terror. Virtue without terror is fatal. Terror without virtue is impotent. The terror is nothing but justice, prompt, severe, inflexible. It is therefore an emanation of virtue."

Maximilien Robespierre 1793

An hour after receiving his summons, Mike Stoodley was ushered into the Cabinet Room of 10 Downing Street. Its long table usually accommodated a cabinet of more than twenty members. As all cabinet members except Sheila were dead, their seats were occupied by those she had appointed to carry out various tasks.

Mike glanced around the room. It was a hive of activity. He noted the presence of Johnny Hammond and Jack Brewer, both of whom seemed uncharacteristically rattled. He nodded to both of them.

Sheila looked up, noticing that he was wearing his piratical eye patch. "Ah, Mike! Welcome. You're just the man we need."

She shooed her personal assistant from the chair next to her, to make room for Mike. "I've declared myself interim Prime Minister and we're trying to assemble other survivors to form an interim government. Meantime, I've been issuing Orders in Council; they have the force of law. Sadly, we have no council, but never mind that for now. I've declared martial law and a lot of other things. I'm scripting a speech for my BBC broadcast in an hour. Get Johnny Hammond and Jack to brief you. They've been invaluable and I'm rather busy right now."

Mike caught the glance between Jack and Johnny, as they ushered him into an anteroom and chased out those working there. He thought he should be cagey with these two. They were sound men but not insiders to the plan. Mike said, "Well, Sheila hasn't changed. How did she survive and get here? I've been pulled from my sick bed. What am I supposed to do?"

Jack and Johnny gave each other another glance. They needed to be sure of Mike. They knew he had been at Essex University with Sheila. Johnny opened. "We don't know too much. Everything's a mess, as you can imagine. We need to get to the surviving junior ministers and MPs. She seems to be assembling them at RAF Northholt, west of here."

"We still haven't been able to find the air unit that brought Sheila Reynolds here. They left immediately afterwards. GCHQ is trying to find out who they were. They are trawling their records of all data and phone traffic to understand what happened to her in Hertford."

Mike grunted, pretending to be conspiratorial, "That's all a bit odd. Maybe we need to keep an eye on her. In my line of work, I hear a few things."

He caught another look between the two of them and continued, "I've called in all my people and we are checking our channels and sources to see what we can find out. We're already in touch with our contacts in MI6, MI5 and GCHQ to pool information. We'll get the bastards who did this."

***

When Johnny Hammond and Jack Brewer arrived at RAF Northolt, they found an increasingly unruly crowd gathering in a hardened hanger. The big doors that allowed access for aircraft were closed. Such buildings, built to withstand bomb blasts, could be completely sealed in case of biological or chemical attack. The hanger had its own air purification and filtering systems.

As they entered, a military police sergeant major checked their IDs. He ticked their names off on his list.

Jack and Johnny entered the hanger together. They saw a large screen, with rows of seats facing it. Some of the people in the room were seated and chatting. A few were remonstrating angrily with the military police guards at the doors. The MPs had instructions not to let anyone leave. They were politely giving everyone the same line. "Yes, sir, we understand that you are anxious to leave. We know how important you are. Our orders are that we need to keep you in here, where it's safe for now. When proper accommodation is secure elsewhere, you will be offered transport." The rest of the throng was milling about in various groups and engaged in animated discussions.

Johnny Hammond noted the familiar face of the Archbishop of Canterbury in deep conversation with the
Bishop of Bath and Wells. The Archbishop was wearing a tweed suit with just a purple shirt and white
clerical collar to denote his calling. Jack remarked.
"We need to keep an eye on him, too. His MI5 file
shows that he was at Essex and he had far left lean-
ings, though his opinions seem to have swung to the
right over the years. Archbishops of Canterbury are
usually either closet lefties or too tender hearted to
be of any use to man or beast."

The two new arrivals automatically scanned the faces,
as they were trained to do. Conferring occasionally, they noted at least eleven members of Parliament, who had been absent from the Abbey. One
was on a stretcher and attended by a pretty nurse.
She was changing his intravenous drip, hanging from
its portable stand. The others must have been away
from the funeral due to bereavement or various other
pressing or personal issues.

There were a few generals, including Major General
Roberts, called in from GCHQ. He was looking worried and gave Johnny and Jack a wave. Various admi-
rals from bases outside London, an RAF air vice mar-
shal, and many lesser ranks made up the rest of the
large military contingent. The leaders of several major trades unions were present, as were several peers

from the House of Lords. These included a couple of billionaire industrialists, who could not attend the Royal funeral at the Abbey.

An RAF group captain, with the toecaps of his shoes highly polished, marched smartly in front of the big screen and bellowed, "Quiet please! Ladies and Gentlemen, please take your seats. The BBC broadcast is about to begin." The crowd broke up and people took their seats, some of them grumbling noisily to their neighbors.

Sheila's BBC broadcast was back-projected onto the screen. She was well turned out and dressed in a smart black suit. She looked straight at the camera and began, "Citizens of Great Britain, you know me. I am Sheila Reynolds. I am sad to tell you that I am the only surviving member of the British Cabinet, in which I was the Home Secretary."

"Whoever is behind the awful events of the past days tried to kill me too, but here I am. I am acting as interim prime minister, until we can restore order and elect new representatives of you, the British people."

The Archbishop of Canterbury jumped up from his seat in the hanger and shouted, "On whose authority does she get to be prime minister? She was responsible for national security."

The first sea lord, in his full admiral's uniform, commanded, "Be quiet! Give her a chance."

The Archbishop glared at him, but sat back down.

An opposition MP chimed in, "We should have been consulted!"

One or two others barracked her, as though they were in a typical rowdy debate in the House of Commons. There were shouts of "Here! Here!" until they were shushed by others, straining to hear Sheila over the din.

The new prime minister continued and softened her tone, "All of you who have lost loved ones will get help. The whole British nation shares in your suffering." She paused and dabbed her eyes with a handkerchief, as if in tears.

"We are proud of the brave men and women who are helping those in need and maintaining our security at this awful time. We know of the personal sacrifices that you are making to stay on duty."

Then she looked more severe and to the rising consternation of Jack Brewer and Johnny Hammond, said, "I have received reports that these atrocities that have so tragically killed and maimed thousands of our men women and children, were plotted by traitors and terrorists in the UK. The plot includes industry leaders and some of our own military and security services. Be assured that we will not rest until these terrorists and murderers are caught and brought to justice."

Johnny muttered an aside in Jack's ear, "Where the hell did that come from. We've been told nothing."

The prime minister continued in slow and measured tones, pausing between each sentence. "In the meantime, stay calm. Stay off the streets. Keep away from public places. Do not join any mobs or groups on the street. They will be severely dealt with. Do not spread rumors and gossip. I will keep you informed as much as possible."

"Following this message there will be a list of emergency numbers to call to register or find missing persons. Please only call them if you have a need. There will also be locations and schedules for emergency food distribution."

"We in Britain will rise above this disaster. The spirit that saw our great country through the Blitz in World War II and that has built this great democracy over hundreds of years will rise again. We must all strive to rebuild and safeguard our country. We will become a prosperous, peaceful and better society. Let us all work together towards this."

The broadcast over, a BBC newscaster started to give the numbers and details that the prime minister promised.

A hubbub broke out in the hall. Those attending started to discuss what they had heard. Johnny whispered to Jack, "What the hell does she know? Why weren't we told?"

Jack rejoined, "Something here isn't right."

They noticed that a dissident crowd was gathering around the Archbishop of Canterbury. They separated and walked over to it, staying on the fringes, ears straining to hear the discussions. The group included a few military men, including General Roberts, some peers and members of parliament. The Archbishop was saying, "Look, we need to act together. She's part of the government that allowed this to happen. We need a representative council, as soon as possible. All those who want to be involved, give me your business cards. When you get out of here, gather like-minded people and I will get in touch with you." He collected a stack of cards.

Jack and Johnny did not hand in their business cards. Why put their interest on record? They decided to contact the Archbishop on the quiet.

* * *

In the next days, several internet sites appeared. Some proposed a takeover by a newly energized British National Party, 'The New BNP'. They called for street demonstrations, especially in immigrant areas. Mike was privy to these web sites and related tweets. Those interested were to meet at various abandoned industrial plants in large cities.

* * *

In a disused warehouse in the industrial city of Birmingham in England's Midlands, beefy bouncers had checked each person entering, against a list, before locking the doors. The New BNP leader harangued the angry crowd, gathered inside. He spoke through an amplified megaphone. Tough looking skinheads with barely sentient amphetamine eyes formed the bulk of attendees, which was ninety percent male and one hundred percent white. He began his oration. "We all know who caused all this! It was those skiving immigrants and Moslem jihadists.

His face working with hatred, he spat out, "We've all seen what happens when you put them on the dole, give them free houses and let them take the jobs belonging to white people. They're running our cities. They started by taking over our kids' schools and the social services. Now they've taken over our whole country."

"Now is the time to deal with the scum once and for all. Tonight we march on their slums! We'll burn the swine out and slaughter them all!"

The crowd cheered and waved their fists as he continued. "The time has come for us to act. We have put up with years of weak government. Now those black bastards have blown up everything we stand for, democracy, freedom and our beloved Royal Family."

A tough looking man, with a beer glass scarred face and a broken nose at the front, yelled his approval, "Yeh! They killed the fuckin Royals. We'll fuckin kill them."

The leader smiled benignly at him, held up his hand for silence and continued. "Now we say, 'Enough!' We say, 'This ends here!' We say, 'Now we will get rid of them all!'"

There was wild cheering until he held up his arm again. "I want you all to get in your vehicles and go to where the ISIS and Al Qaedas live. You know where they live, hiding among women and kids, pretending to be peaceful. Now we'll slaughter 'em all, women, kids the lot. Burn them out! No mercy!"

The skinheads started a rhythmic, wild and mindless chant, "Kill the wogs! Kill the scum! Kill the blacks. Kill the scum. Kill the Pakis! Kill the rats! Kill the Yids...."

His mouth set in a grim line, Mike Stoodley saw the pictures of all this. They were beamed directly from the helmet camera of former SAS Captain Benjamin Kossoff, currently leading 'Operation Sarah' for Mike. Kossoff was looking down on the scene, hidden in a mezzanine office in the warehouse. He tried to keep calm as he heard the Nazi style invective and chants. He could smell the sweat rising from the tightly packed mob below. He could feel the waves of venomous hatred rising too. His grandparents and most of their generation had perished in the Holocaust. It took all his self-control to keep his finger from the trigger of his weapon.

Fortunately, Mike spoke directly into his peoples' earpieces. "That's enough, lads and lasses. Open Fire! No survivors."

He added a thought. *'This is for you too, Sarah.'*

High in a steel truss above the mob sat ex Royal Marine Sergeant Damanjeet Singh. His pale blue turban contrasted with his all black combat gear, but it was masked by a black hood. He gently squeezed the trigger of his GPMG, General Purpose Machine Gun. He controlled it as it banged and bucked into noisy life. Its wooden butt was firmly tucked into his shoulder to avoid it wandering off target. He fired in short, aimed bursts. Brass cartridge cases spewed from its ejector, falling like metal hail on the scene below. At the same instant, others responded to Mike's order, firing downwards from various points in the metal roof beams. The noise was deafening, due to the confined space and the corrugated metal roof.

Bullets stitched a hail of lead from side to side and all across those below. Some rounds ricocheted, sparking off steel stanchions and sending chips flying from the concrete floor, bouncing up into the legs and groins of the mob. Most rounds simply shredded bodies and splattered blood, mashing internal organs. The once baying mob was torn apart by high velocity 7.62mm rounds. Some bullets passed through three or more bodies, shattering bones and leaving massive exit wounds.

They kept shooting till the last broken body stopped twitching, avoiding touching their searing hot gun barrels. Then 'the boss', Kossoff, who reported directly to Mike Stoodley, and seven others climbed down and walked around below. They administered a head shot to each corpse, just to be sure, reloading their 9mm Beretta M9s with fresh magazines multiple times.

In his report to the next meeting at number 10 Downing Street, on this and several similar events, Mike commented, "That should keep the fascists down for a bit. If not, we'll do it again."

* * *

A week later, Jack Brewer and Johnny Hammond met in the bar of the Old Grey Mare pub in London's Fleet Street. They wore civilian clothes and checked the other drinkers carefully to spot anyone unduly interested in their conversation. Everyone looked normal, but professional spooks would look like this. Jack spoke softly. "Well then, Johnny, let's pool what we've found out."

Johnny took a sip of his beer, "I found no records of one of our choppers bringing Sheila Reynolds to Downing Street. Even in the chaos, someone should have filed the paperwork or at least had a memory of it."

"There's worse," said Jack. "A mate of mine in Hertford nick told me they found a right mess outside the town. Smashed up cars in the road and four bodies all shot in the forehead. They still carried their protection squad warrant cards. Their pistols lay by their sides, unfired and with no rounds in the chambers. They were murdered in cold blood."

"A farmer reported that someone stole one of his tractors and crashed it. He saw a man running off and getting away on a scrambler type motorbike. The escort must have trusted whoever did it. Why?"

"Shit!" exclaimed Johnny. Some of the drinkers looked up. He calmed himself down.

Jack said, "Wait. There's more. Blood tests at the hospital, where Mike Stoodley was supposed to be recovering from a heart attack, showed he might have faked it, using amphetamines. The results mysteriously disappeared, but an assistant in the path lab remembered."

"So we have our first suspects and they're running the country. What the hell do we do now?"

* * *

The Archbishop arranged a clandestine meeting of as many of the dissidents as he could muster. It was held in a basement room at his official London residence, Lambeth Palace. He asked those invited to arrive at staggered intervals, so as not to arouse suspicion. He was quite pleased with the haul.

* * *

Jack and Johnny arrived separately as they had agreed. They were careful not to be seen together and went to different places in the room, so that they could observe the proceedings. They were very much on the alert.

Everyone was waiting expectantly. A trembling deacon walked up to the podium and stammered nervously into the microphone, "The A-a-archbishop will be a-along s-shortly. We'll s-shut the doors n -now, for s-security." He then rushed out by the nearest door. The heavy locks could be heard clicking in the massive oak doors. The room was sealed.

Too late, Johnny heard a hissing. His military training kicked in and he automatically shouted, "Gas! Gas! Gas!" There were of course no gas masks to cram hurriedly on.

All the militarily trained people in the room looked desperately around them. No member of NATO trained forces had escaped being trained on how to put on a respirator in seconds, when their instructor shouted "Gas! Gas! Gas!" Some delegates scrabbled at the unyielding, locked doors and fell in heaps around them.

Johnny desperately held his breath and clasped a tissue over his face, but it was ineffective and too late.

Finally he was forced to breathe in. One by one, everyone in the room collapsed. He thought, *'So this is how life ends.'*

As he fell, Jack Brewer groaned his wife's name, before everything went black.

Half an hour later, as fans were turned on to clear the gas, teams of men, in white boiler suits and wearing respirators, entered the room. They began loading the bodies into sealed trucks for transport.

CHAPTER 14
PREVENTING OUTSIDE INTERFERENCE

"There are no borders in this struggle to the death...... Each spilt drop of blood, in any country under whose flag one has not been born, is an experience passed on to those who survive."

Che Guevara

Six months after the destruction of Westminster Abbey, Acting Prime Minister Sheila Reynolds chaired a meeting of her Foreign Affairs Committee. Acting Foreign Affairs and Security Minister Mike Stoodley and Minister of Social Policies, Archbishop Phil Saunders were also present. Phil and Mike attended all key meetings, regardless of the subject.

Sheila opened, "Now Mike, please update us on the current international situation. Is there anything we should worry about?"

Mike acted his part, as one of the team trying to save the country, after the disgraceful terrorist events perpetrated by others. "There are plenty of things we need to worry about, but on the whole things are going quite well. The key fact is that we are not being threatened with attack, which was what we expected by now, before this all started."

"As expected, the liquidation of most of the world's leaders in the Abbey led to chaos around the Globe. The purpose of this seemed to be partly to offer other governments the opportunity to rebel. This seems to have worked in some countries at least."

"Fortunately, the hot heads, especially in the US and Russia were stopped from nuking those they felt 'might' have been responsible. Bombing Israel or North Korea would have started a world war." Even better, we are not on the list of suspects. We are the primary victims."

"Our secrecy, swift restoration of order here and spreading of positive information means that everyone is still trying to understand who was responsible. They are behind our interim government. Opinion polls show we have eighty-five percent backing for tough action."

"So far, France, Spain, Italy and most of the eastern part of the European Union have all declared alliances with us. Our meetings with their new leaders are resulting in some harmonization with the policies we have announced so far. We've arranged for the elimination of one or two suspect leaders. My special forces teams have played a leading role in this, so far without detection."

"The Rump EU crowd in Brussels is still meeting regularly. With their funding cut off, attendance is thinning out. The revolutionaries clearly helped promote riots and the sacking of the EU parliament buildings. Most member states have severed their EU connections to focus on their internal problems."

"There's vicious fighting in Germany between the neo-Nazis and the left. We are covertly supporting the left to keep the Nazis out, but their civil war is keeping attention away from us. We aren't in a hurry for it to end."

"The US is an utter shambles. The country is split between Republican states, demanding secession and the Democrat states, massing to fight for the union. Amusingly, that is a reversal of the two parties' positions in the American Civil War."

"Russia is kept busy with several attempts at separation by its Islamic populations. Fascist type regimes have seized some of the other cities in its constituent states. Feeding their people is going to be their main problem. Most countries have dealt with that by declaring martial law and strict rationing. In Russia widespread fighting in many conurbations means it's not working."

"The Chinese are the biggest surprise. They've simply closed their borders and are redeploying their population to focus on food production. As I told you last week, they marched into North Korea too, worried at having a loose cannon on their doorstep. 'The Exalted Leader' is confirmed dead by the way. Sources say he was hacked to death and eaten raw by a starving mob."

* * *

Two weeks earlier, in the White House Washington DC, a vituperative meeting had ended in chaos. Lou Donatelli, the Secretary of the Treasury, shouted at his colleagues, "Look, as the attorney general just said, the succession rules are clear. The President and the Vice President are dead. The current president should rightly be the president pro tempore of the senate. He's disqualified himself by fleeing to

Austin and declaring himself President of the Republic of Texas. Next in line should be the Secretary of
State, but he's dead too. I'm next in line! That's the
law!"

Joe Charlton, the Secretary of Defense, yelled back.
"Look, Lou, be pragmatic. Neither of us was elected
by the people. We are under threat from many countries. The Chinese and Ruskies are just waiting for the
opportunity to attack us. They are likely behind this
whole thing anyway. It's my job to stop that. Face it.
We need to do the job together! I know it's a new idea,
but this is an unprecedented situation."

The Secretary of the Treasury looked directly at the
head of his secret service detail. "Listen, you heard
the attorney general. I'm the President. I'm ordering
you to arrest Joe! Now!"

The Attorney General tried to calm things, but Joe
socked Lou in the jaw, and Lou's secret service team
started shooting. Both contenders were cut down in
the crossfire. Within seconds the succession was now
down to the Secretary of Agriculture. She burst into
tears.

* * *

Mike called Sheila on a scrambler phone, as soon as he received the news from Washington. She listened to his report with a wintery smile. "So what do you expect to happen next, Mike?"

"Well, a pattern is emerging. In these chaotic times, large federal states, like those of the European Union, the US, Russia and India are unable to control their component parts. They're breaking up along long standing fault lines."

"The power is going to those who can quickly deliver more local solutions. Suspicion of non-locals and central governments is overwhelming. State governments are taking local control, except in some of the big cities. The mayors of Moscow, Chicago and New York have seized power and declared martial law and strict curfews."

"Much of this fits our expectations and thinking. We've always felt that government, taxation and policy decisions should be made as close to the people as possible."

"There's more news from the US, too. At Fort Knox, Kentucky, fierce fighting broke out between the 16th US Cavalry Regiment and what could be loyal federal troops, though it is difficult to be sure anymore. It seems that the US gold reserves were seized on the orders of a Major General Dimmock. He's a Texan and was in the Skull and Bones Fraternity at Yale, with the new president of Texas. Federal drones and Apache gunships were still attacking his troops when we last heard."

"As you know, the world financial markets and global economy have effectively collapsed. There is as yet no way to put them back together. The World Bank, the IMF and most financial institutions have locked their doors. Their leaders have fled to take care of their families. Only strong state control can work in the short term. Those commanding forces on the ground are in power. We've taken the necessary steps and others are doing the same. Each country is operating as a closed economy for now."

"Being more prepared than most, we've opened a UK Sovereign Wealth fund in the City of London. We're buying up high quality assets at knock down prices, in countries where we expect order to be restored first."

"Mostly as we predicted," exulted Sheila. "And even better in some cases. Well, that gives us the breathing space to build things the way we want them. I'm calling for elections in two months. That will legitimize our regime."

Chapter 15
Separating the Wheat
from the Chaff

*Progress is impossible without change.
Those who cannot change their minds cannot change anything.*

George Bernard Shaw

**Extracts from A History of the Isle of Man,
By J. Y. Peters, published in 2030**

*"The Isle of Man is equidistant from Eng-
land, Ireland and Scotland in the middle of
the Irish Sea. It is just over 30 miles long and
14 miles wide.....*

In both the World Wars of the 20th Century, large numbers of enemy aliens, political prisoners and prisoners of war were interned in camps on the Island....

Since the Sheila Reynolds government put an end to the forces of revolution, several assessment and rehabilitation centers have been in operation. They deal with those suspected of crimes against the good of the people and revolutionary acts. They are housed in ultra -modern facilities. Many attendees at these centers are given wide-ranging freedom, after initial assessment.

Also situated on the Isle of Man are the evaluation centers for those who wish to be qualified for top jobs in the UK. These include all candidates for pay grades 1 to 7 in the Civil Service; all service ranks above and including captain in the Republican Navy, colonel in the Army, group captain in the Republican Air Force and chief inspector in the Police. Candidates for parliamentary constituencies and all ministerial appointments in the government are included. All board members and the top three levels of executives in corporations, partnerships and charities, with more than 10,000 employees must pass the assessments too.

In effect, these programs have become graduate schools, controlling access to all leadership roles in Britain. This started with the first post-revolutionary elections, where sixty percent of would-be candidates were eliminated after assessment...

These centers have been studied and emulated by other countries around the world. Employment and the Isle of Man's economy have boomed. This was due to the construction of these facilities and the resulting employment of custodial, assessment and training staff as well as visitor traffic. Jobs in these activities successfully replaced the pre-revolutionary reliance on offshore financial services. They were formerly the mainstay of the Manx economy. All financial activities other than those for Manx domestic use were closed during the Revolution and not reinstated under the post-revolutionary government of Sheila Reynolds."

* * *

Some years before *A History of the Isle of Man* was published, professor of psychology and head of senior assessment for the British government, Professor Bruce Mackenzie, looked balefully at the pile of candidate reports on his desk in Douglas, the Isle of Man's main town. He had moved there with his family from his previous academic post at the Durham University.

He was feeling tired. The realization that he had eight interviews with senior candidates for the next day left him feeling drained.

Each candidate report included the results from a battery of psychometric tests. There were also reports on each candidate's behavior in the group exercises. Body language results on each subject were considered extremely important. The output from the new Israeli software that analyzed the hidden 'tells' from micro expressions, which indicated lying, was especially useful. The candidates were unaware that they were being filmed throughout the assessment process. Other software synchronized their facial expressions with individual answers in the psychometric tests and noted those answers where they were untruthful.

The professor personally reviewed the files on all top-level candidates and interviewed them. He probed those areas where other assessors had felt there was doubt. Fortunately he had a faculty of highly trained staff to deal with the thousands of other senior appointments.

All candidates in the post-revolutionary elections had been assessed, including the triumvirate of Sheila Reynolds, Phil Saunders and Mike Stoodley. The professor was pretty sure that very few unsuitable people had been elected to Parliament. In those cases where he harbored doubts, he felt sure that the government would correct any mistakes. He was concerned about one candidate in particular, but Mike had set his mind at rest.

***

He remembered how Mike Stoodley persuaded him to take on this fascinating and important, but extremely debilitating, challenge. It was at a meeting with Mike in his study in Durham. He had a copy of the government's proposals in front of him, in a file marked 'Top Secret'. He was flattered to read many of his own ideas and theories supported in the document. He also had major concerns. "Mike, you have to remember my professional ethics."

Mike was charming, as always. "Of course, Professor, please explain any ethical difficulties with the ideas that we've been discussing."

"Well, for a start, it's unethical to evaluate and test a subject, without the person knowing what the tests are meant to evaluate and what the results will be used for. Normally, our patients are with us because they want us to help them. They give truthful answers."

Mike interrupted him. "With respect, Professor, sometimes your profession has often evaluated whether sociopathic criminals can be released back into the community. At that point, the patient's rights should always be secondary to those of the general public. In too many cases the murderers, rapists and robbers committed other crimes and created more victims when they were released."

"Well, alright, I'll grant you that. In such cases, we are also aware that they may well be trying to deceive us. The most important other objection I have is the covert surveillance elements in this proposal. I agree that they add significantly more accuracy and validity to the results, but secret filming and recording conversations outside the test facilities is like Orwell's *1984.*"

Mike looked him in the eyes. "Well, Professor, this is simply a question of the greater good argument."

"How do you mean, Mike?"

"It's very straight forward. If you want a country run by sociopathic elites, you support the ethics of your profession. If you want to ensure that those in power and administration care for the people they serve, then you bend your professional ethics for the greater good."

* * *

Jack Brewer and Johnny Hammond were among the few declared suitable for further senior employment from the many who had been brought there from Lambeth Palace. The after effects of the fentanyl-derived gas had been slight. Both awoke glad and rather surprised to be alive. They had feared that lethal cyanide or sarin was being used, as they had lost consciousness.

In the lounge bar of the Jolly Sailor pub, in the village of Ramsey on the Isle of Man, Jack and Johnny were in a heated political discussion with several others. They had all received positive assessments. All tested low on the continuums for sociopathy and narcissism. There were civil servants, a couple of potential politicians and some business people seeking promotion. Johnny and Jack both kept back their particular knowledge and involvement in the days of revolution.

Walking home from the pub, Johnny asked, "Any word on the new appointment you were promised, Jack?"

"Still waiting. How about you?"

"Nope! All I get is, "Be patient. We see you as a key resource. The various classes you are attending will be needed in your new role."

"I get much the same. You don't think they are just stringing us along?"

"I don't see why they'd do that. If they suspect us of knowing too much they'd just bump us off. They must need us for something. How are your courses going?"

"Well, we're sharing the ones on public finance; taxation and business studies, so I'll just talk about international politics and sociology. In short, they are eye openers and I enjoy them. It does seem that our previous masters kept us in the dark with lies, half-truths and spin. I'm learning as much from the other students as I am from the program. They have all sorts of interesting experiences. Still, I need to get back to something productive. This place is driving me barmy."

"It's the same for me, Johnny. I'm especially enjoying the legal programs, but I need action. Also the wife and kids are going a bit stir crazy here. They're keen to get back to London. You seem to be doing OK here. The new regime is favoring female candidates. You always have a pretty one in tow!"

Ignoring the last remark Johnny rejoined, "Mmm, you have to wonder if they are scared we'll reopen investigations into the murders and explosions. On the other hand, why all the education if they wanted to ditch us?"

They continued their conversation as they walked along. Jack stopped and pointed upwards, "Wait a minute! What's that?"

"Ah, it's a mini-drone, exactly like the one that appeared when the Abbey blew up. They're all over the place. I've been waiting for this."

Johnny pulled a stout homemade catapult from his pocket, inserted a ball bearing into the strong elastic and pulled it taught. When he let go, his eyes gleaming with satisfaction, the drone shed smashed shards of green plastic, swerved out of control and crashed onto the roof of a nearby house. Then he continued speaking as if nothing had happened.

"I hope you're right about them having a use for us, Jack. At least they didn't ship us off to Anglesey with all the sociopaths!"

As they went off to their separate accommodations, Johnny discretely pressed a folded paper into Jack's palm when they shook hands. Jack slipped it into his pocket without showing any acknowledgement.

* * *

Former bank chairman Ronald Jessop and his wife were bickering over early morning coffee in their small cottage. It was on the storm swept island of Anglesey, off the coast of Wales.

Ronald complained bitterly. "What pisses me off the most is that they think we can live like this. Look at this coffee mug! It probably came from a bloody supermarket. They don't seem to understand. We're accustomed to fine china and servants."

Margot Jessop spoke sharply to him. "So what are you going to do about it? You should be planning to get us off this damned island and away to Texas. Cousin Freddy loves living in Austin. I really hate working in that miserable chicken processing plant every day. It's full of stupid peasants. The smell is horrid. I don't ever want to eat chicken again. The pop music they play on the loudspeakers is quite appalling and so loud. The work is ruining my hands. You can't even get Chanel creams here."

"Oh shut up, Margot. It's a lot better than the farm work I have to do. At least you're in the dry. It's always raining here. Some of us do discuss getting off the island, but it's surrounded by stormy seas and in many places some enormous cliffs and vicious currents. The locals aren't a bit sympathetic either. Some of them just want to humiliate us. My foreman lost his pension in some scam. He seems convinced it was all my fault. Some days he refuses to even talk to anyone not speaking Welsh. Silly sod!"

"Besides, the bridge is heavily guarded. Joe Abernethy told me that two people were shot dead last month, trying to get across. Poor old Rupert Smyth -Witham ended up in Long Lartin maximum security prison for not toeing the line"

"Can't we bribe the guards?"

"What with, a stolen chicken?"

"Well, you'd better sort something out! If you hadn't tried to hide our money when they questioned you, maybe things would have been better?"

"You absolute bitch, Margot! You were the one who was very keen on keeping our financial secrets. Anyway, we just need to bide our time. Just you wait. They'll soon see they can't run the country without the likes of us. It's in our blood. Then we'll pay the buggers back!"

"Alright, I suppose we have to wait. Meantime, here's a letter from the boys."

"Gervaise complains that the food and beds are even worse than at Eton. They're being bullied by some rough boys from Leeds. They even have to do their own washing and cleaning. George Rupert seems to be accepting it more than Gervaise."

∗ ∗ ∗

Jack crept into his house and softly looked in on his sleeping children. He took a torch into the back garden and shone it on Johnny's handwritten note.

> *"We need to meet to plan next steps. They seem to have cameras and microphones everywhere. The pub is not safe. Let us meet on the beach, tomorrow at the usual time and place."*

He lit a match and held the burning note up till it neared his fingers and then let it float away. He looked around him and then went indoors to slip into bed beside the sleeping warmth of his wife, careful not to wake her with his chilled body.

∗ ∗ ∗

In the surveillance control center, in Peel on the Isle of Man, an operative watched the live video stream of Jack's surreptitious trip to his back garden with interest. The infra-red camera zoomed in on Jack. He hoped he would get the blurred picture of the torch-lit note enhanced overnight to see what it said. Meanwhile he reported his observations up the chain of command.

Jack and Johnny were on a special surveillance list. Because of their counter measures training, a team of twenty-three, some acting as fellow students, were assigned to watch them. Recording devices and cameras were hidden in all their regular haunts. The latest micro tracking and listening devices were even woven into their clothing.

* * *

At noon the next day Jack and Johnny met on the beach as planned, having carefully approached by circuitous routes. Only a woman walking a dog a hundred yards away was in sight. Jack smiled at Johnny, "Right! Time for a swim."

They both completely stripped off and raced each other through the chilling surf. "Fuck!" said Jack, "The water's freezing!"

"Fuck!" muttered the duty surveillance man in Peel. Then he spoke into his headset. "Can you do anything, Jane?"

The dog walker responded, "Sorry, Boss, they are in the sea and my long range antennae is only picking up the sounds of the surf. How about the drone?"

"I'm trying to maneuver it to an oblique angle, so we can get a lip reading, but I think we'll be too late."

* * *

At his desk, Mike was reading the request from Jack and Johnny for a face-to-face meeting. He had reviewed the transcripts of their recent interactions. Intrigued, he looked up at his PA. "OK, arrange a plane. I'll go and see them tomorrow afternoon."

* * *

Mike walked into the grey-walled meeting room, past the Marine guards, acknowledging their salutes with a nod. Jack and Johnny were already seated, having walked through the screening frame without incident. He smiled at them. "Gentlemen, how can I be of service?"

Jack looked sternly at Mike. "Thanks for coming, Mike. We asked you here to answer charges of treason."

Showing no surprise, Mike relaxed his hands on the table and laughed. "Well, that's taking a risk. You saw the guards outside."

Johnny and Jack unsheathed the long, razor sharp ceramic chefs' knives from their hiding places in the smalls of their backs and held them in a firm grip pointing towards Mike. Johnny had manufactured the knives on his home 3D printer, using a low carbon material only detectable by the most sophisticated scanners. The one in this facility was old. Mike made a mental note to get it changed. Johnny said, "You know you'd be dead before they made it into the room. I reckon we could take them out too."

Smiling and disturbingly unflustered, Mike said, "That makes sense. What's the plan? You get me to whistle up a chopper? Where do you think you can go?"

Jack replied equally calmly, putting their conjectures on the table as facts. "Never mind that for now. Let's talk first. We know you weren't in the Abbey, because you faked a heart attack. We know Sheila arranged the ambush on her convoy to avoid being at the funeral too. We know she was delivered by one of your copters and her escort was murdered. Together with the Archbishop, the three of you planned and executed the whole thing. What do you say to that?"

Relaxing back in his chair Mike responded, "Well, well! You are clever chaps. Let me explain why."

Jack and Johnny were astonished that there was no denial and that Mike remained calm. Mike took well over an hour to explain most of the reasoning behind the revolution. Both gripped their weapons, their knuckles showing white as the tension mounted. They realized Mike would not be so forthcoming if he planned to let them leave the room alive.

Mike concluded his description of the events and planning leading up to the seizure of power, "Sheila, Phil and I have the greatest respect for both of you. Your loyalty, intelligence and capabilities will be needed in the future. That's why you have been interned and trained here."

Minds racing at this unexpected statement, Johnny and Jack saw that they might get out by feigning co-operation, but Johnny had to fight down his rising anger, remembering the slaughter of so many of his men around the Abbey. Setting his knife down with slow deliberation, but within easy reach on the table, he said, "Well, what's your proposal?"

"Our proposal is that you continue to be prepared and stay here just a little while longer. Then you'll be brought to London to help build the future."

Baffled, Johnny looked at Jack. He saw Mike press one of his cufflinks and he grabbed at his knife, but a radio-activated needle in the chair injected him in his left buttock, as Mike leapt out of his reach. He growled with frustration, as the fast acting drug floored him. He saw that Jack was down too. They had lost all ability to move, but remained conscious.

Mike smiled down at them. "Sorry, chaps, I'm too old to be quick enough to deal with you any other way. You will return to your studies. We know you'll try again, but my advice is to wait till you're called."

He left the room. Then a medical team came in to deal with the two poleaxed men lying on the floor.

CHAPTER 16
SUCCESSES AND FAILURES

The history of any nation follows an undulatory course. In the trough of the wave we find more or less complete anarchy; but the crest is not more or less complete Utopia, but only, at best, a tolerably humane, partially free and fairly just society that invariably carries within itself the seeds of its own decadence.

Aldous Huxley

Eight years after the revolution, there was an important meeting at the prime minister's country residence, Chequers Court, in Buckinghamshire, England.

Mike pushed the heavy oak door into the meeting room and found Phil and Sheila already there. They were in heated discussion. "Look, Sheila, it's been eight years and we've only delivered half of what we expected to by now. It's just not good enough! Every time I want to spend money on essential social programs, you block it. Maybe you should step down."

"How dare you speak to me like that?" shrieked Sheila, her voice raising a few octaves. "I'm the fucking Prime Minister! We're all doing our best. Our budget is tight. Maybe it's you who should go. Fuck off back to Paraguay!"

Mike quickly stepped in, pulling a Hepplewhite dining chair up to the highly polished table. "Now, now, boys and girls, let's all calm down, before we say things we might regret. We're here to discuss progress and next steps. Let's do it calmly and slowly."

Sheila grunted, still seething. "OK, Mike, why don't you start then? For Christ's sake, start with something positive."

"Well, Phil has a good point. We are behind schedule, but let's review our achievements so far. There's much to be proud of."

"Firstly, we eliminated the ruling elite, confiscated its wealth and rehabilitated those capable of redemption. All this was without the blame for the necessary violence falling on us."

Sheila interrupted, waving a finger at Phil. "That's hardly a minor achievement."

Mike cut in before Phil could object. "Quite right, Sheila. What's more, we created the Sovereign Wealth Fund to manage the confiscated finances. It's doing rather well after a slow start. The world was full of cheap assets due the global chaos. Now things are finally picking up. It is projected to grow at twenty-five percent per annum over the next few years. That should pay for lots of social programs, Phil. It also comfortably beats the long term record of most pre-revolutionary private capital funds and hedge funds."

Only partly mollified, Phil commented. "Fine, but the world economic crash destroyed forty percent of our economic output. We're only now recovering. It took time to replace the fat greedy bastards in business with better people. At least we've proved once and for all that leaders don't have to be paid hundreds times more than the workers to be well motivated. Your employee trusts partnerships are world -beaters."

"Good point." broke in Mike, regaining control. "It is a definite achievement, retaining a market economy, but with a significant amount of the capital in some of the large enterprises owned by the Sovereign Wealth Fund. The employee-owned trusts work well and they certainly motivated the workers to stay on our side. Small stockholders in the confiscated enterprises were compensated and most people were happy to see the fat cats simply stripped of their wealth."

"The initial collapse of the economy also led to many entrepreneurial businesses stepping into the gap. They're generating a lot of the resurgence. That's fine too, as long as they don't become too large and their leaders too greedy."

Sheila, never quiet for long, blurted out, "In my opinion, a major achievement was avoiding outside intervention. Better still, there are now many countries with similar regimes to our own. The global free trade initiative between like-minded regimes will take time to get going, but the seeds are planted and sprouting."

Mike said, "Also, the move back to democracy went smoother than we thought. Our Democratic Unification Party is immensely popular. The assessment centers are just great. Well done to you, Phil, for your part in setting them up!"

"Thanks, Mike, but what's the story with your Big Brother style surveillance? I hate feeling that every time I'm in bed with someone, every grunt and gasp is being listened too and noted by some pervert in a bunker. You promised to fix this."

"So I did and so I have, Phil. Part of the reason was to stop others using drones and intercepts against us. You'll find that new limits are quietly being set for all such operations. Only in the case of terrorist suspects can we target homes and then only with an order signed by a judge. We are setting limits on the number of these any judge can sign in a year."

They went to dinner in a more relaxed mood and Sheila drank even more than usual. Mike managed to ward off her amorous advances, as he had for many years. He was more than happy to leave her to bed her young lovers.

Over dinner, Phil asked, "Whatever happened to Lady thing with the Rembrandt? Remember, her husband was a greedy banker."

Mike laughed. "That's a good tale. She started a torrid affair with the manager of the chicken factory, and not long afterwards her husband was found dead in suspicious circumstances. Unfortunately for her, we keep very close tabs on all the sociopaths and she was easily found out. We had a voice recording of her plotting the whole thing with her lover. They're both serving life sentences now. I hear that she's having a fling with the toughest of the prisoners in the female maximum security wing."

As they left the dining room, Mike left them with a parting comment. "There's something rather delicate that we need to discuss. I'll bring it up when we're all fresh in the morning."

*　*　*

After a light breakfast of fruit and cereal they headed back to the meeting room. Phil had insisted that the senior members of the government should eschew the fine dining and luxury of the old regime. Mike was always frugal in his own lifestyle. Sheila had given them the most trouble, but finally acquiesced, at least publicly. She had plenty of separate opportunities to sate her appetite for the finer things in life, away from Phil and Mike's annoying scrutiny.

Sheila opened the morning meeting with "Come on now, Mike. Don't keep us in suspense any longer. What's the delicate matter you wanted to discuss?"

Mike looked each of them in the eyes in turn and said, "It's time that we take a good look at ourselves. Each of us has surrounded ourselves with strong teams. We have excellent cabinet colleagues, whom we still keep outside our inner circle. They are starting to get frustrated by that. The bottom line is that we should be thinking of vacating our roles."

Sheila looked quite distraught. "Hang on a minute, Mike. I love this job and I do it well."

Phil let out a long sigh. "Course you do, Sheila, but Mike's got a good point. I've been wondering about raising the same issue. The problem is we are too damned old."

Sheila instantly overrode them. "Speak for yourself, Phil. I certainly won't be giving up so easily."

Mike said, "Let me show you this video and then let's see what you think."

* * *

As was Mike's habit, he had sent out his people to conduct analysis on the state of the nation. The video was interlaced with the usual interviews with people around the country.

The opening shots soon had Sheila and Phil squirming uneasily. There were new aircraft in a private hanger at Biggin Hill Airport. Interviews with the business people using the planes in the passenger lounge were especially worrying. A finance director remarked, "Well, we could use scheduled flights, but we really need the peace and quiet afforded by these small personal jets to gather our thoughts for important decisions."

The elegantly dressed CEO of a pharmaceutical company was travelling with her personal assistant and tennis coach. She said, "Look, as long as we are discreet, we deserve the luxury of getting over to Paris for a little R and R once in a while. I deserve this, because we are really successful."

Mike paused the video. "Does all this remind you of anything?"

"Bloody hell!" exclaimed Phil, "We're right back where we started."

"Not quite," said Mike, "But we have a growing problem and it needs to be dealt with. Let's watch the rest of the video."

At the end of it even Sheila appeared disheartened. The film showed luxury restaurants, hotels and resorts. There were exclusive golf clubs and sports facilities. Some clips showed senior executives getting out of large chauffeur driven cars. An advertisement for an expensive international travel firm, offered exclusive holiday packages. After a half hour or so, Mike paused the video again. His two colleagues looked embarrassed.

"You've seen no ordinary people so far. What you are seeing is the new elite. The next film clips are showing how most people are coping and what they think of all this."

Phil and Sheila were even more disturbed by the contrasting lives of the majority. Their comments were very direct. Effectively, they approved of the post-revolutionary reforms and the benefits they brought, but felt things were slipping back to the way they were before.

Sheila said. "That's quite enough, Mike. We get the message, so what should we do?"

Mike said, "The day we always talked about is now!"

Phil nodded, but Sheila went white.

* * *

As the meeting broke up, Mike flashed a signal to Phil to stay behind. After Sheila was well clear, he shut the door. "There's something I need to show you, Phil."

He put his index finger on the touchpad on his red dispatch box. It checked his fingerprint and unlocked itself. He passed a file, stamped 'Top Secret', to Phil. "Read that."

Phil started to read and looked up at Mike, shocked. "Jesus, Mike. Is this real? If it is, why've you kept it from me?"

"It's real all right. You, Professor Mackenzie and I are the only people who've seen it. That's the only copy. I kept it from you because we needed to finish the job. If that got out, we couldn't have done that."

Phil looked at him steadily in silence and then said. "I suppose I can understand that. Why show it to me now?"

"Because it's time to do something about it."

* * *

Johnny and Jack were taking what had become their weekly swim in the sea, screened from surveillance by the sounds of the waves.

Johnny spoke through the breathing of his strong breaststroke. "I know we both agree with a lot of what's been done, but I'll never forgive those bastards for killing so many people, especially my men."

Swimming beside him, Jack said, "I agree, but we need to let them think we are on their side, so we can seize them and bring them to justice or, more likely, just do them in. They didn't give those around the Abbey any kind of trial. We'll need a lot of others to join us to get it done though."

"That's a problem, said Jack, "They've got everyone under surveillance. So far, this is the only place we can talk. Mass swimming groups won't work and anyway, how can we trust anyone?"

Johnny answered. "OK all we can do is play along, take our new jobs and then build a cadre of loyal supporters. It'll take time, but how else can we do it?"

"Sorry to say, I see no other way either, Johnny. Let's do it then. Anyway, I'm going blue with cold, I need to get back to the beach."

CHAPTER 17
A SURPRISE

*"No government power can be abused long.
Mankind will not bear it"*

Dr. Samuel Johnson

A couple of weeks later, on a Thursday night the happy hour crowd in the Admiral Nelson pub in Shepherds' Market was enjoying strong real ale. The large LED screen hanging on the wall was showing a World Cup soccer match. England was losing to Costa Rica in the second round. Those not talking together were glued to the screen. There were futile encouraging shouts to the far distant players. "Oh, come on, England! This is like a replay of 2014. How can such a tiny country beat us again?"

Then the match suddenly disappeared and a stern voice interrupted their libations. "This is the BBC interrupting your program. Stand by for an important official emergency announcement."

The hubbub around the bar and tables gradually subdued, as some drinkers drew others' attention to the screen. Suddenly, the familiar chamber of the People's Meeting Hall appeared. It had been built on the site where Westminster Abbey had stood. Its cavernous auditorium was filled with the usual serried ranks of Britain's leaders. The pub goers could see that they included the upper echelons of the military, internal security services, civil service, trade unions and the various religious groups. Unusually, many foreign leaders were also present.

One drinker gave the finger to the screen. And another, worse for drink shouted, "Fuck those bastards!"

He was shushed by others, as the camera panned to the stage. There stood the three top people in the nation, all looking very serious. Mike Stoodley, Defense and Security Minister, was flanked by Phil Saunders, the Archbishop of Canterbury and Minister for Public Health and Welfare, and Prime Minister, Sheila Reynolds. The Prime Minister appeared to be trembling a little. Mike Stoodley was wearing his signature black eye patch.

Another inebriate in the pub guffawed. "Hey, look, they're holding hands, the wankers!"

Indeed the three leaders seemed to be gripping each other's hands very tightly. The prime minister took a breath, stopped shaking and broke the clasped hands. She held up her arms to silence the ritual applause from those in the auditorium.

She spoke in solemn tones, without any of her usual smiles. "Today, I am speaking live to the leaders of our country and to our international guests in this assembly hall."

"More importantly, I am speaking on television and via live links especially to the people of our country. Those overseas who followed our recovery from revolution and receive this broadcast around the world should also be interested in what we have to say."

"Eight years ago, revolution brought tragedy and death. Those here in this hall and you, the British people, recovered and rebuilt from that. It was hard and everyone made sacrifices. Together, we generated tremendous change for our great nation. Perhaps it was the most important change in the last thousand years. The world was in chaos. In some countries maybe there was too much change. History will judge these things."

"During and soon after the revolution, many of you suffered great hardship. We had to eliminate or re-educate the dominant elites that had plotted the revolution. The bloodsuckers were leaching off the hard work and sacrifice of the mass of decent people. They were embedded in every part of government and industry. Democracy had become a sham. Most people didn't bother voting because it was a waste of time."

"Because of your hardships and your efforts, we have delivered on Rousseau's dream of liberty, fraternity and equality. You have all seen great benefits."

There were murmurings of assent around the pub, but one woman squawked, "What about you fat cats then?" A few others muttered their agreement.

The prime minister continued. "Mike Stoodley has an important announcement to make as to the future."

The more sycophantic attendees in the auditorium started clapping again. She silenced them with a glare. "There is nothing to clap about. Listen to Mike!"

Mike took a step forward. "We were always aware that post-revolutionary regimes end with new, self-serving elites replacing the old. In many historic revolutions, monsters came to power. Think of Napoleon,

Hitler, Stalin and Mao. Look at the mess the United States got into after the idealism of its revolutionary war. It attempted to act as arbiter of world affairs purely in its own interests. This has led to wars, murders and failures, well into this century. All these regimes were responsible for tens of millions suffering pain, famine and death. In each case, their revolutions aggrandized the leaders' own positions and power and that of their cronies."

"Even in the case of the post-revolutionary government here, already we see new power elites starting again. This is true in both business and government, indeed throughout our society."

Some in the auditorium cried, "No! No!" Others looked shiftily at each other.

Mike gave them hard stares and waited for silence. "Here in Britain, those in leadership roles have tried to get preference for their children, friends and relatives. They have accumulated privileges, like special cars, luxurious offices and lavish entertainment. They have gone back to the old corrupt habits of offering favors for favors."

Many more in the auditorium fidgeted with embarrassment. Others looked grim and stony faced, balling fists or gripping the arms of their seats.

Mike continued, "We were aware of this danger from the outset. We planned for this day. Now is the time for a change! There will be announcements next week of new elections."

A beery voice cried out in the bar, "So more of the same then!"

This was reflected by looks of relief and murmurs from the hundreds assembled in the People's Hall. Mike held up his hand to quiet them. "Wait! I haven't finished!"

Slowly he transfixed his audience with a cold gaze from his one good eye. Firmly seizing the hands of the prime minister and the archbishop, who stepped forward either side of him, his voice rose. "We have done all we can!" He raised their clasped hands upwards to form two Ws. He felt Sheila's sweaty and trembling hand. Phil's was dry and firm.

"We here have all become the problem. Others have to take over for the future. We hope that when their time comes they will do as we do. If not, they should be overthrown by you, the people of Britain!"

Those in the auditorium and the pub were united with surprised looks and some gasps. "What on earth?"

Then, inside the hall, explosions erupted thick and fast. Before the screen went blank, the three on the stage disappeared in a flash. They had smiles on their faces. The heavy concrete ceiling of the People's Hall started to fall, crushing everyone in side.

The pub goers sat in silent shock. One inebriated man bawled, "Mine's a pint of whatever Mike Stoodley was drinking!"

CHAPTER 18
AN ENDING
AND A BEGINNING

*"No enterprise is more likely to succeed than
one concealed from the enemy until it is ripe
for execution."*

Niccolo Machiavelli

"As the concrete ceiling of the hall collapsed, Mike, Phil and Sheila were already leaving the underground car park in a black Range Rover. It was one of the new driverless ones that were finally becoming available after years of safety problems and public nervousness.

Sheila was flushed and exultant, "That was a bit fucking close, Mike! I thought you were really trying to kill us," She laughed with relief.

Mike smiled and remarked, "It's amazing what can be done with a forty second delay on the broadcast and an inserted last scene."

Mike glanced at Phil meaningfully. "Have a brandy, Sheila. Steady your nerves a bit."

* * *

A week earlier, Mike and Phil had been in deep conversation with Sheila in 10 Downing Street. Mike finally conceded, "OK, Sheila, Phil and I have talked things over. You're quite right. The country needs continuity. Just because we must remove the new elite of fat cats, doesn't mean we have to retire."

Sheila breathed a deep sigh of relief. "That's great, Mike, I thought I'd need to have you both dealt with. We're different from the others. We don't need to obey the same rules as everyone else. My destiny is to see this through. Somehow, I need to survive and to continue as Prime Minister with the new team."

Mike gave Phil a furtive glance. Sheila was so wrapped up in her self-belief that she missed it. "Sheila, let me organize our escape and a safe house west of London, where we can hole up for a day or so. Then we simply drive back and resume leadership."

"Thanks boys, I'll leave the details to you. Now pour me a stiff brandy!"

* * *

As they drove on to the M4 West, she savored a second drink from the cut glass crystal brandy balloon from the cabinet in the back of the Range Rover. Then she fell asleep in her seat. She never woke up.

Phil said, "So she was a sociopath all along. What did Mackenzie say in that file? *'Absolute belief that she is special....Rules don't apply to her....Desperate to win and keep hold of power.'* Well, Sheila, you really had me fooled.'

He glanced regretfully at her rather bloated body. "I guess you were right to keep that file from me, Mike. We did need her to achieve what had to be done."

"Well, Mackenzie called her a 'functioning sociopath.' She was necessary to hold things together, but I swore to him that we'd deal with her when this point came. He's a good man. He wanted to be in the hall back there, but the new people trust him. He's an austere man committed to public service and no fat cat."

"What'll you do now, Mike?"

"It's best you don't know exactly, Phil. There's a village I came across in a remote place in Africa when I was in the SAS. I'll try to teach the children a little and help as much as I can. I did some bad stuff there. I need to make amends.

"What'll you do when you reach Paraguay?"

"I'll raise a few chickens and maybe do a little teaching too."

∗ ∗ ∗

Jack Brewer and Johnny Hammond, together with about sixty others were spread among three luxury buses, driving east from Northholt RAF base towards London. They had a large police escort. No one noticed Mike's Black Range Rover, as it passed at speed, on the opposite carriageway heading towards Brize Norton RAF base.

The military police captain in each bus checked his synchronized watch. Simultaneously, they spoke into each coach's PA system. "All right, ladies and gentlemen. Listen up! Sorry for all the cloak and dagger stuff, but you can now open your sealed orders."

Jack and Johnny were in adjacent seats. "Well, well," said Johnny as he started to read. "They've done it again. The people on these buses are to take over."

Jack replied, "You have to admire them Johnny. At least we don't have to arrest them as we'd always planned. Let's try to continue their good work, but no more killing eh?"

"There's always killing, Jack."

The End

Author's Perspectives

The Pennine Chain is a range of hills, which forms the spine of England, dividing the East from the West. It runs from near the Scottish Border to the English Midlands

The description of Todmorden and the lives of those living there at that time are based on my own experience of the town. As a boy, I lived there for a while with my grandparents.

It is a typical mid-Pennine town. It lies in a valley, a narrow pass squeezing between the hills. Many things are crammed into this slender space, besides factories and dwellings.

There is a cricket pitch. My Grandfather was obsessed with cricket. In retirement, he dragged me along. Matches used to last for days. To me it was like watching paint dry.

Brass bands were another northern passion. My grandfather, a cornet player, passed on his love of music to me. Many of the old bands are gone, with the factories and coalmines that supported them. The film *'Brassed Off'* excels in portraying such a band.

A canal runs through the town. It used to connect with the national network of canals. When canals were the cheapest form of transport for coal and much else, this 'Rochdale Canal' was a vital link across the Pennines. Some of my kinfolk worked for the canal company. There are flights of wooden locks to enable barges to climb the high passes.

The River Calder passes through the valley too. It sometimes floods, but is usually more of a shallow stream at this point.

There is also a narrow and twisting road. It is frequently blocked by snow in winter. It used to be the main route between Manchester and the industrial towns of Yorkshire, Halifax, Sheffield and Leeds. There is still a lot of traffic, but the four-lane M62 now bypasses the town, high above the moors and funnels most of it elsewhere.

British Railways replaced the smoky steam trains with diesels after I left. The line emerges from a seven

-mile long tunnel just west of the town. We boys re-moved the light bulbs in the carriages to make mis-chief in the dark. I can still smell and taste the smoke and soot inside the carriages. As the coal burning trains passed under bridges they left a trail of chok-ing smoke. Sparks sometimes ignited the dry grass along the railway embankments.

Stoodley Pike was and is a well-known Todmorden landmark. It was funded by public subscription to mark the victory over Napoleon I. It is truly a bleak spot on a rainy day. From there, you can still look down and see grand homes that belonged to the mill owners and those houses for their workers that were not later condemned and demolished.

Many of the massive mills still stand, minus their tall chimneys that belched smoke. They had their names painted around the top. The spinning, dyeing and weaving has all gone to Pakistan and other cheap la-bor countries. Now, some mills are used to house small enterprises and offices.

Todmorden today is a much cleaner town than in the 1950s, when I first knew it. The open stretches of the canal are for pleasure barges and fishermen. Ducks and moorhens still forage among the reeds, just as they always did. Seagulls still winter on the canal, away from the stormy North Sea.

The pollution from smoke ended, as the mills closed and coal fires in houses were forbidden. The river, just upstream in nearby Walsden, no longer changes color according to the dye works' production on any given day. Todmorden's sooty buildings have largely been sand blasted to their original yellow sandstone.

* * *

My grandparents were variously Irish, Scottish and English. Three of them spent some or all of their lives working in the cotton mills. My maternal grandmother started working part time at age nine and full time at twelve. She was deafened by the clattering of her four looms in the weaving shed. She worked near her sister, who tended the next four looms. They learned to lip read to overcome the din.

My great grandfather, her father, lost both his legs and lived at home, alternately cared for by my grandparents and his other daughter. My grandfather suffered an industrial accident at work.

My paternal grandfather came from a family of petty criminals in the neighboring town of Rochdale in Lancashire. He died before I was born, estranged from his family.

You can see, that coming from a long line of peasants, I was very lucky to have a loving home. Free education for all is no longer available, but for many of us baby boomers it offered the first opportunity in our families of university education. In my case, I was fortunate to have been able to have an international business career.

Sadly, the same opportunities are rarely available today. Social mobility has retreated rather than advanced. Nearly half the British population gets a degree of sorts, but the high paid jobs are no longer on offer.

* * *

I chose Essex University because the excellent Canadian economist, Richard Lipsey, was head of the school there. He and his faculty taught me a lot. Another reason was that it took me far from home. I was a rebellious teenager and have changed little.

Whilst almost all of the people in this book are fictional, some are not. They include Professors Peter Townsend and Richard Lipsey, worthy academics, who taught at Essex in 1967 and beyond.

John Major was the pathetically ineffective British prime minister who followed Margaret Thatcher.

David Triesman was a student leader at Essex, during the sit-ins and other unrest during 1967 and 1968. Like most rebels, he later joined the establishment. He became a junior Labour Government Minister, was ennobled as Baron Triesman and is a member of the House of Lords.

Other characters are a blend of types that could be encountered at the University of Essex between 1967 and 1970. Still others are composites from later experiences. The campus and student life at Essex were much as described. Many of the incidents in this book occurred as written. Tom, the cartoonist, was viciously satirical. His style was similar to that of Gerald Scarf. There was a witch-hunt for him, over the Royal Cartoon. The police were desperate to get their hands on him. If they did, the author never heard news of it.

* * *

The 1968 'protest marches' or 'riots', depending on your viewpoint, took place in London and Paris almost exactly as recounted. I marched and was otherwise 'active' with the anarchists. At least one demonstrator was killed by a baton round in Paris, as described. Some rioters simply disappeared.

I knew a member of the Angry Brigade quite well, but only afterwards heard of their exploits. The person portrayed in this book is fictional.

I was beaten and taken behind the police lines in Grosvenor Square. It was far from deliberate, rather painful and in retrospect well deserved. There was an attempt to turn me into a police informer after an arrest on a minor charge, but I did not betray friends.

***

The partial history of Gayhurst Court, where our protagonists plotted, is accurate. The house was also a secret base for breaking the enigma naval codes, in WWII. Then it was an annex to the much more famous Bletchley Park and focused mostly on U boat codes.

Gayhurst House figures in history books and several novels.

***

Much has been published about the increasing concentration of wealth and power in the hands of elites, since I started this book in 2012. This is excellent timing.

The elites do control governments and businesses. Wealth is passed from generation to generation. Many now agree that happenstance of birth; genes or circumstance are the major determinants of wealth. Luck is the overwhelming factor. Many successful people are convinced that their success is entirely deserved.

There appears to be no peaceful way to break the mould. The elites ensure that that is the case, determined to pass it all on to their heirs and so on far into the future.

* * *

The British Media and its target audience mostly love the Royal family and celebrities. The Hanoverian Succession, as described by Johnny Hammond, is accurate. The Royal family of today succeeded through a very distant relationship and is heavily of alien, especially German, origin. Tradition is its only logic.

Relevant Reading

Some of these authors inspired many students at Essex and elsewhere in the late 1960s. If you want to understand what helped foment the rebellious mood, read some of them.

Great Fear in Latin America, John Gerassi, 1965

Revolution in the Revolution, Regis Debray, 1968

The Motorcycle Diaries, Ernesto Che Guevara. These were more recently made into an excellent film.

These are more modern books that explain much, with the advantages of hindsight:

Che Guevara: A Revolutionary Life, Jon Lee Anderson, 1997

Pinochet: The Politics of Torture, Hugh O'Shaughnessy, 1999

The Real Odessa: How Peron Brought the Nazi War Criminals to Argentina, Uki Goni, 2003

Guy Fawkes or The Gunpowder Treason, William Harrison Ainsworth and George Cruikshank, 2011

The Beginning of the End France 1968 What Happened Why it Happened, Angelo Quattrocchi, 1998

1968 in Europe: A History of Protest and Activism, 1956 -1977, Martin Klimke and Joachim Scharloth, 2008

The Angry Brigade, a History of Britain's First Urban Guerilla Group, Gordon Carr, John Barker and Stuart Christie, 2010

The Girl in the Picture: The Story of Kim Phuc, the Photograph, and the Vietnam War, Denise Chong, 2001

Vietnam: A Complete Photographic History, Michael Maclear, 2007

Revolutions: A Very Short Introduction, Jack A. Goldstone, 2013

A very British revolution 150 years of John Lewis, Johnathan Glancy

Unwarranted Influence: Dwight D. Eisenhower and the Military-Industrial Complex, James Ledbetter, 2011

To help understand two of the locations, these works are relevant:

A History of Todmorden, Malcolm Heywood, Freda Heywood and Bernard Jennings, 1996

Living With the Wire: Civilian Internment in the Isle of Man During the Two World Wars, Yvonne M. Cresswell, 2010

With excellent timing, the next book has become an international best seller:

Capital in the Twenty-First Century, Thomas Picketty, 2014

Hopefully it will make this novel more credible. I started this book in 2012. Picketty has been massively, and so far ineffectually, attacked by the elites and their apologists.

He proposes wealth taxes. In my view, global wealth taxes will never happen. The embedded elites will stop them. If a single country decided to heavily tax its billionaires, they would simply move elsewhere. The prospect of all governments acting together is much less likely than the events in this novel.

Revolution may be the more realistic alternative. The danger is that populist, right wing, fascist parties will take control.

There was an excellent Guardian Newspaper *Report on a study of global wealth inequality* by Oxfam published in 2014. Oxfam is an excellent charity. The report is a splendid explanation which is causing people to think more about the injustices of extreme wealth inequality.

www.theguardian.com/business/2014/mar/17/oxfam
-report-scale-britain-growing-financial-inequality

Oxfam's latest wealth report 'Even it up', published in
November 2014, is available at

http://policy-practice.oxfam.org.uk/publications/
even-it-up-time-to-end-extreme-inequality-333012

BOOK CLUB QUESTIONS

This book is unlikely to appeal to those refined and genteel souls that comprise most book clubs or those focused on pulp fiction. Hopefully, there are others with a burning interest in politics and social justice.

Why do you think the author wrote this book?

Are the popular opinions favoring celebrities and the British Royal Family portrayed in this book an accurate portrayal of popular culture?

Have you encountered sociopaths in business or politics?

To what extent are the major democracies manipulated by the political and business elites?

Do former activists change their spots when they become part of the political and business establishment? Can they retain their original intentions?

Short of confiscation, is there any realistic way in which greater equality can be created other than by revolution?

Is the graphic violence in this book a reasonable description of the horrors of revolution?

At what point, if any, do the risks and suffering from a revolution become acceptable?

What would it take for you to rebel?

Status of other books by Aaron Aalborg

They Deserved It

– Is partly a historical novel and partly set in the present. It is based on the true story of young 17th Century Italian women forced to marry rich old men. It will appeal to all those who like strong female characters, historical drama and dramatic twists and turns.

In a conspiracy led by an older and wicked woman they use slow poisons to rid themselves of their husbands. They are caught in a trap set by a cunning pope and variously burnt at the stake tortured and hanged. This scandal set the whole of Europe ablaze. Every husband feared for his life.

By means of the mysterious contents of an ancient Egyptian casket, the story then moves through their descendants to modern day New York. Amidst political intrigue and a wild global chase the story partly repeats itself.

It is published by Penman House Publishing and is currently available from Amazon as a paperback or as an e-book.

Terminated

– This thriller will appeal to all those who have been fired and anyone who is disillusioned with the misuse of power and corruption in big business and has lain awake at night dreaming of revenge.

It is a novel about the evils of big business, firing and deadly revenge.

A high flyer rises from humble origins and becomes disenchanted with the food industry, banking and many other businesses, despite being enormously successful. He fires many employees during his rise to success.

He is eventually sacked from his job, as Chief Executive, by his board of directors. Over a long period and in unexpected ways, he hunts down and terminates all those he deems were responsible for him getting fired.

Terminated is in currently being written and will be published by Penman House Publishing in early 2015.

The Destroyers

– This is a thriller is about a frightening conspiracy theory that could already be true. It describes how a mysterious organization uses black ops to deal with all who are deemed to be threats to the US government.

This is rarely by assassination, but more commonly by interference and sabotage of the victims' daily lives, using the latest technologies. These methods are already available and if they are available, you can be sure they are being used.

A group of young rebels strikes back against tremendous odds, with dramatic and terrifying consequences.

The Destroyers is scheduled for publication in late 2015 by Penman House Publishing.

Black Smoke White Light

Black Smoke White Light is Aaron Aalborg's project for 2016. It will bring the World of Eastern spirituality and contemplation into sharp contrast with the forces of evil in the modern United States.

'Smoke out light in' is a Tibetan Buddhist meditation technique. David Roberts spends twenty years in Tibet overcoming the inner demons of his youth. He develops immense spiritual powers that can influence his surroundings.

When humanity is threatened with unspeakable horror, his abbot sends him on a mission to the now unfamiliar and horrifying world outside the peace and tranquillity of the monastery.

Projecting his astonishing mental focus outwards, he meets and overcomes the forces of darkness in a series of thrilling and startling encounters with the twisted and wicked people trying to destroy civilization for their own ends.

On behalf of Penman House Publishing
and the author,
thank you for purchasing this book.

Additional Penman House titles from:
K. Francis Ryan
Are available from Amazon.com.

More information can be found by going to:

PenmanHousePublishing@gmail.com

Aaron Aalborg is a nom de plume. The Author was born near Todmorden in Northern England and educated in Rochdale and Manchester before reading Economics at the University of Essex and management at the Victoria University of Manchester. He has degrees in Economics and Business.

He had military training and an international career in business. As a result, he met and observed many leading politicians, corporate titans and the machinations of governments at first hand.

His other interests include current affairs, psychology, history, politics, Scottish country dancing, tai chi, Buddhism and edible fungi.

He and his wife have lived in Europe, Asia, the US and Latin America.